THE DESTROYER!

What does CURE, the world's most secret crime-fighting organization, do when it comes up against the impossible mission?

They create the perfect weapon—a man, Remo Williams. He is convicted and condemned to death for a crime he didn't commit, and is then practically resurrected from the dead—programmed to become a cold, calculating death-machine.

And Remo Williams is a success at his job of destruction. An enigma to everyone but his fantastic mentor, Chiun, an Oriental wizard and warrior, he outperforms all the heroes of yesterday and today—truly the superman of the eighties!

The Destroyer #4

WARREN MURPHY & RICHARD SAPIR

MAFIA FIX

P

PINNACLE BOOKS
WINDSOR PUBLISHING CORP.

This novel is a work of fiction. Names, characters, places, and incidents are either the product of the author's imagination or are used fictitiously. Any resemblance to actual events or places or persons, living or dead, is entirely coincidental.

PINNACLE BOOKS

are published by

Windsor Publishing Corp.
475 Park Avenue South
New York, NY 10016

Sixteenth printing: September, 1988

Printed in the United States of America

For the family whom God made sweet—the Van Sluyters of Melrose—David, Jean, Mark, Blake, Sue, Mary, Beth, and E.G.F., who always had our respect, and now that we don't work for him, also has our affection.

CHAPTER ONE

It was a perfect trap.

It had been sown in the flowering fields of Turkey during the wet, warm spring and it bloomed briefly in the back streets of Marseilles in July, and now it would be harvested in the muggy heat of late August on Pier 27 of Hudson, New Jersey, "gateway to the nation," as it had been called when the nation had looked only to Europe for its culture.

Now, via Europe, it was importing death in bricks and bars and bags to be sniffed, skin-popped or mainlined into the veins of Americans.

A glassine envelope with only a trace element of an ounce was worth $5 to the person who wanted to murder himself with it. A plastic lunch bag big enough for a slice of cake or a school lunch sandwich was worth $15,000, an uncut brick of it was worth as much as $100,000, and a suitcase of it might be worth millions.

Sometimes two valises would come in, and if seized by the authorities, the news would be splashed across the front pages of the nation's newspapers: $9 Million seized or $16 Million seized, Biggest Haul Ever, Nab Record Drug Cache.

By the ounce it was worth more than gold. And

adding the bags and valises, the false bottoms in suit-cases, the holes in statues, the hollow heels and money-belts full, it came into the bloodstream of America by the ton. But never more at one time than a couple of suitcases full. Never more, as far as the Treasury Department knew, until a dying man whispered to an undercover narcotics agent in Cleveland, Ohio, about the big one.

When the big one came, you would be able to buy it by the pound at two-thirds of what you were paying now. When the big one came, the little wholesalers would be wiped out. When the big one came, you would get it in pills, in serum bottles, in cigarettes, all pre-packaged as it had never been packaged before.

You could buy a franchise in June for delivery in September. You could get the stuff with any label you wanted on the cover devices. And you could get all you could sell when the big one came.

Another informer in San Francisco told about the big one. And in Dallas and Miami and Chicago and Boston and Detroit and New York, the signals kept filtering through to the local narco squads, to the state police, the FBI and the Treasury Department's narcotics unit. The signals said that the big one is coming in August and by the time the first football is kicked off in the first high school football game, there will be enough to turn on every cafeteria, office, street and home in the nation.

That's how big the big one was.

And that was the first mistake.

As an assistant attorney general of the United States pointed out in a secret conference in Washington: "What the mob is doing this time is the equivalent of the Viet Cong leaving the countryside and deciding to fight a set battle at sea. Gentlemen, we've been given the first real break in our war against the drug traffic. They've come to play in our ballpark."

On an international level, the first steps were easy. Intelligence-gathering is a dull accounting process of examining pictures and charts, markets and large-scale movements of things. For an army to move anywhere, gasoline, men and trucks must begin to roll. On a large scale, the indicators might be the sale of grain, a rise in the price of oil, the scarcity of cigarettes. Nothing big happens without the indicators.

And for the big one in heroin, there were plenty of indicators. The harvest would require the agricultural production of half a nation and the first indicator was the almost immediate drop in unemployment and starvation in that nation. The price of farm labor went up. The price of grain went up. Fields that had grown wheat for centuries were no longer planted with wheat. You didn't have to stand fifty miles outside of Ankara taking photographs of fields to realize that wheat as a crop was being abandoned.

You could read it in the *New York Times* listings for the commodity markets. Grain shipments to Turkey. You compared that to the weather reports for the region and when you found out it was very good growing weather, you knew something was being grown besides grain.

You could walk through the food stalls of Ankara and seeing the rise in prices for all produce, know that what was being grown was not for eating in Turkey. You then checked the agricultural exports from Turkey and, seeing no rise, you knew their farmers were not exporting grains or fruits.

Thus, even if the narcotics outlets hadn't leaked

the word about the big one, the United States government would still have known about it.

"At last, they've made the big mistake," said the assistant attorney general.

And as the Central Intelligence Agency kept its nose to the periphery of the big shipments from Turkey to Marseilles where gummy, dark-colored commercial opium was distilled into refined, white powder, the State Department pressured Elysee Palace to keep its police away.

"Yes, the United States understood France's desire to free itself of the stigma of being a clearing house for heroin.

"Yes, the United States understood that such a big arrest would vindicate France.

"However, did France understand that this was a singular opportunity to deal a severe blow to the traffickers in the United States; that the big one had to go somewhere, and that at that somewhere must be the top people, whose arrests would cripple the flow of illegal narcotics, not only in the United States and not only in France, but all around the world?

"And, of course, if France persisted in its plan to make arrests at the Marseilles heroin factories, it might be necessary for the United States to send a public note of protest to France condemning it for interfering with a United States plan to deal a mortal blow to international drug traffic. The international press might even hear a rumor that France seized the heroin to protect United States distributors.

"Wouldn't it be so much simpler if France were publicly lauded for its fine cooperation in the big arrest?

10

"France is always willing to cooperate? Of course. Allies again and forever."

So the trap was set, good and tight and big, and on that hot muggy morning at Pier 27 in Hudson, New Jersey, the trap was ready to be sprung.

Inspector Vincent Fabia said the special prayer he had been saying since the spring. "God, let me have this one. I'll never ask for another. This one. Let me have this one."

He waved to the private guard at the gate and eased his green truck with the wooden window flaps and the yellow painted sign saying "Vinnie's Hots— Best Dogs on the Pier," over to the guard who held out his hand as if to shake. Vinnie reached down out of the cab and grasped the outstretched hand with his left. The guard smiled and waved him through. It was a five-dollar smile, the amount of the rolled up bill Vincent Fabia had passed with his left hand and had been passing every day, with few exceptions, for the last three weeks.

It was the small "vig" that was the rule of life in Hudson, New Jersey. A guard at the gate, a shop steward here, an assistant sanitation inspector there, all of whose friendship was necessary if you sold hot dogs from an open truck. And of course, if you sold hot dogs from a truck, you didn't always have the money to pay and you'd plead short every so often, promising to double up the next time.

Occasionally, Vincent Fabia would smile at the thought of his selling hot dogs, just as his father did; just as his father paid off to earn his living in Boston by giving money to the Irish cops who would call him a guinea and take his money and free hot dogs and free cigarettes. All the old man's money was going to

11

put his son, Vincent Fabia, through Fordham. Vincent Fabia, who did not become a doctor or a lawyer or an accountant or a professor, but a cop who was a cop who, when he heard the Italian names linked to organized crime, would squirm in his stomach and vow that one day he would make the big bust with his name right out there, giving the world both vowels at the end of it.

Vincent Fabia, inspector of the United States Treasury Department, who drove his green hot dog truck on to the edge of Pier 27, and parked it as he had parked it for the last three weeks, began to heat the big kettle with the oversized frankfurters, opened the flaps on the sides of the truck and looked out at the most beautiful scene he had witnessed since his wife presented him their first-born son.

To his left, the Panamanian registry Santa Isabella, which had just docked this morning, stood in sharp relief against the New York skyline across the Hudson. Directly in front of him was the long asphalt field where empty truck frames sat in a long string. Within a few days, truck-sized containers would be hoisted from the hold of the Santa Isabella and placed carefully on the back of the truck frames. Then cabs and rigs would be attached and the sealed and locked containers, their contents untouched by human hands on this side of the Atlantic, would be on their way out into the mainstream of America.

Vincent Fabia knew that the two containers he was after would be there this day. Not because intelligence reports told him so. His stomach told him so. "Today is the day," it said, and no computer could tell the mind of Inspector Fabia otherwise. Today was the day he and his men had waited for.

O'Donnell and McElaney would work the hold. They had their longshoremen cards. Hester, Baker and Werner were drivers and assistants. They would be arriving soon to wait for their cargo and they would be there for the entire unloading operation, since in Marseilles their containers were the first to go into the hold. So they would be the last to get their cargo and they would hang around waiting and complaining, but mostly waiting and watching.

In the office building to his right were his reserves, Needham and Viggiano. They would move only if ordered to by Fabia, or if Fabia were dead. In the meantime, they sat there behind a camera, with telephoto lens and high resolution film, ready to pick up identifiable images at a great distance.

Stretched out along Routes 1 and 9 were unmarked Treasury cars. On standby, without exact knowledge of what the standby was for, were the state and Hudson police. The FBI was available for call and "directional reinforcement," which was a nice way of saying that if you fouled things up, they would attempt to unfoul it.

Vincent Fabia, in tee shirt and chinos, straightened out his small formica counter at the side of the truck and added fresh napkins to the dispenser.

He checked the small mustard container on the counter, and seeing it only half-full, filled it. He put out the relish. He opened the heating bin of the sauerkraut and gave it a stir.

The ice in the soft drinks was packed right. He shut the lid on the ice. The straws were adequate.

So was his .38 police special. So was his little transistor radio that he kept plugged into his left ear and which he accidentally had unplugged every day now

13

for the last three weeks so people would hear that it was playing music. Today, it was not playing music and it would not be unplugged.

"It's coming out first. A triple shipment," a voice crackled over the radio.

Fabia clicked his fingers as if hearing a beat. Three containers. Three truckloads and up until this the biggest hauls had been suitcases. The beat went on.

A shiny metal truck container came out of the hold of the Santa Isabella, connected to the end of cables and chains attached to a derrick bolted on the ship.

Containerization. The new way to ship. Four tractor rigs filed into the Pier 27 waiting dock. Needham and Viggiano would pick them up with the telephoto lens for evidence, license plates, company names, everything.

"I said no mustard, you stupid bastard."

Fabia looked down. A longshoreman was looking up angrily at him from the counter. He had given the man a hot dog without realizing it and had drenched it with mustard, also without realizing it.

"Take that frigging radio out of your ear and maybe you'll hear people."

"Yeah, sorry," said Fabia. "I'm sorry."

"I'll eat it, but I won't like it."

"I'll give you another one."

"No. I'll eat it. But next time, like listen, huh?"

"Sure thing. Roger."

"Roger?"

"Uh, thanks. I'm sorry."

"Yeah. Okay."

Relax. That was what Fabia told himself. Pretend this is just another bust and relax. Don't blow it. By tomorrow, you'll be standing in front of the television

14

cameras with those trucks behind you and everyone in the world hearing those last two vowels on the end of your name. Just relax and pay attention.

Slowly, painfully slowly, the crane lifted the first container to full height, paused, then swivelled around and lowered the container onto the waiting truck frame. Immediately, the first tractor rig drove up and began to hitch itself to the truck.

"Don't you want your money?"

"Yeah, sure," said Fabia.

"That was two hot dogs, the specials. And a soda."

"A dollar five," Fabia said.

"That must be some program you got on."

"Yeah," said Fabia and smiled. "Great."

"Second container being readied. There are four in the shipment," came the voice over the radio.

Four? Vincent Fabia smiled at his customer and made sure that he absolutely certainly got the order correct. Mustard and relish on one, sauerkraut and mustard on two and one plain.

"You got onions?"

"No."

"How come you don't have onions?"

"I don't get a big enough call for them," Fabia said.

And the transistor radio—"tall, dark Caucasian, 275 pounds, suit and tie. Standing near containers in the hold. Just looking. Think he's involved. No reason to be here."

"If you had 'em, you'd get a call for 'em."

"But I don't have them."

"Why doncha?"

"Cause I don't get any call for them."

And the radio—"It's definitely four containers.

15

And there are three men in the hold looking around. Well-dressed."

"Hey, I asked for two, not four."

"Sorry. Two, right?"

"Right. With onions."

"I don't have onions. What do you want from me?"

"Onions. You know everybody's got onions. You're the first guy in here what deals from a truck that don't have onions."

"I don't have onions."

The longshoreman's face reddened.

"I know you don't have onions. I'm saying you oughta get 'em 'cause customers like 'em. I'd pay five cents more for onions if you had 'em. Some people just like onions. It ain't against the law. Nobody says you gotta have mustard and kraut on your dogs. Hey! Whaddya doing?"

"What?" said Vincent Fabia.

"Whaddya doing? I didn't order no mustard or kraut."

And the radio—"Number two going up, those men staring at it. They're involved. Maybe we can get them with the telly. Whoops."

"Mustard and kraut, right?" said Vincent Fabia.

"Blow it out your ass."

Vincent Fabia shrugged as a hot dog salesman would shrug, and he leaned down into the corner of his small truck as if to get more mustard. He whispered into a small microphone.

"Did you pick up the deck with the telly?"

"Somebody just passed. That was close. I'll let you know when there's something new. Everything's too close."

16

Vincent Fabia sold 174 hot dogs that morning and eighteen more by 4 p.m. that afternoon. He was literally soaked with sweat. His tee shirt looked as if it had been hosed, and his trousers were two shades darker than normal. His hair hung limply in wet strands; his eyes were red. He felt as though he could neither lift his hands nor his feet; just keep his balance by great strength of will. But when the four loaded tractor trailers with the emblems on them— Ocean Wheel Trucking Company—began to roll off Pier 27, he knew suddenly that he could climb Mount Everest if he had to.

He leaned into the corner of the cab, flicked a switch, and said very loudly:

"Pickles. Pickles. I'm going to get pickles. Got to get pickles. Pickles."

And the signal beginning the close of the trap was out. He shut the flaps of his truck, and for the first time in three weeks did not bother to close the lid on the big mustard jar beneath the counter, from which he filled the small dispenser jar.

He stuffed the .38 caliber police special into his belt and toyed with a line that he might deliver at some communion breakfast—about youngsters having a choice between right and wrong, and no ethnic group being particularly addicted to any special offense, and maybe even how too many people remembered only the Italian gangsters who were caught, not the Italian detectives who caught them.

It was the Mafia and the people who dealt with them who were the fools, not the majority of hardworking Italian-Americans and other Americans.

Vincent Fabia did not get a chance to deliver his speech about who had brains and who didn't. His

17

brains were found splattered on the seat of the cab of his hot dog truck at 3 a.m. the next morning, parked near the cemetery on tree-shaded Garfield Avenue in Hudson, New Jersey. Powder burns surrounded the remnants of an eye socket and slivers of his skull were imbedded in the back of the seat.

Just before quitting time, two longshoremen had been crushed to death beneath a container that slipped its rigging and plummeted down onto them in the hold.

And two office workers, who were photography buffs at an office at Pier 27, left work without taking their camera. They never came back for it. Which was all right with the management, because it never got much work out of them anyway.

The state and local police stayed on alert until midnight and, finally receiving no signal, checked with the Treasury Department.

By dawn they received word to call off the alert, with thanks for their cooperation. They were not told what the mission had been or whether it had succeeded.

They were also informed to be on the alert for any Ocean Wheel Company trailer-trucks. To stop and to search them. They were not told how many Ocean Wheel trailers or what the license plate numbers were. They saw no such trucks.

By 1 p.m. the next day, in the oval office of the White House, the assistant attorney general who had coordinated the operation was explaining to the attorney general, the director of the Federal Bureau of Investigation, the director of the Central Intelligence Agency, the Treasury secretary and a very dour President, what had gone wrong.

"At about 4 p.m., we lost contact with our Treasury agent, and that was it. No traces. Nothing. We are in the midst of a blanket search now." He stood at the far end of the conference table, a sheaf of papers before him, wishing for a mild heart attack. Even a severe one would do.

"You said two tractor-trailers with heroin. How much heroin in each?" This question from the director of the FBI.

The assistant attorney general moved his lips and mumbled something.

"I didn't hear you," said the director of the FBI.

"Full," said the assistant attorney general, forcing out the word.

"Full? From front to back? Two full trailers of heroin?" The director's face was red and he was almost shouting; he had never been known to raise his voice in conference.

"Yes," said the assistant attorney general.

There were groans in the oval office of the President of the United States.

"Excuse me, gentlemen," the President said. "Stay right where you are. I will be back in a moment. Continue this without me."

He rose and strode from the room, down a corridor, up a flight of stairs, and into his private quarters. His wife was napping on a big double bed and she woke her gently, asking to be forgiven, but just as firmly insisting that she leave the room for a moment. When the door was shut, he took a key from his pocket, unlocked a dresser drawer, and brought out a red telephone with a white dot. He looked at his watch, as he lifted the receiver. It should be answered at this time. It was.

19

"Yes, sir," came the thin voice.

"Do you know what happened in Hudson, New Jersey, yesterday?" asked the President.

"Yes," came the thin sour voice. "There were many things that happened. You are probably referring to the shipment from Marseilles."

"Yes. The two trucks."

"There were four."

"Then you are working on it," the President said.

"I should hope so."

"Will you use him? That person?"

"Mister President. Please save your advice for football coaches. I'm busy. Now do you have anything important to tell me?"

"No. No. You have it all. Is there anything I can do?"

"Perhaps. You might try to keep the Treasury and FBI people in that area to a minimum. It might save their lives."

"Then you are going to use him?"

"That is a fair assumption."

"Is he there now?" the President asked.

"He is finishing up a matter elsewhere. He will be there shortly."

"Then you have everything under control?" the President said.

"Is there anything else you wish to tell me, sir?"

— "Please. This is a grave crisis. It would ease my mind if you told me that you have it under control."

"Sir, if I had it under control, we would not be using him. By the way, sir, I have told you there were four trucks. Please do not give that information to anyone else, lest they ask you where you got it and you give them little confidential hints."

20

"I understand," the President said. "I know now that we will solve this crisis. I'm considering it under control."

"If that makes you feel better, sir, fine. Unfortunately, you seem to think that person is a solution to problems, when in reality he is a potential problem of far greater magnitude himself."

—"I don't know what you mean," the President said.

"Good," came the thin voice, and then the click. The President returned the receiver to the cradle and the phone to the drawer, then shut and locked the drawer. He had been hung up on again.

As he returned to the conference, in much better spirits than he had left it, he wondered where the man on the other end of the line had found that person, what his name really was, where he was born and what his life must be like.

But most of all he wondered what his name was.

CHAPTER TWO

His name was Remo.

He tried very hard not to be bored, as if the threat were very real. This was necessary to get the exact information he wanted. The exact information was what he had been ordered to get before he could proceed.

So when the ruddy-faced gentleman in his late 50's casually asked him if he cared to go fishing, Remo had said "yes, that was what he had come to Nassau for."

Then when the ruddy-faced gentleman told him to wear the life jacket for safety and had insisted on buckling it himself, Remo had thanked him. And when the ruddy-faced gentleman guided the small motor launch to a small cove protected from the sweeping breezes of the Caribbean, told Remo that the life jacket was really weighted and the buckles were really reinforced locks and that one stamp of the ruddy-faced gentleman's foot on a gray plug near the stern of the boat would sink it, Remo showed fear.

He screwed his face to tension, opened wide his brown eyes and made tugging motions at the jacket with his strong hands. It did not budge. Good. Now the ruddy-faced gentleman felt secure. Remo could tell that by the smile.

"You bastard," said Remo. "Why have you done this to me?" The ruddy-faced gentleman in gray Bermuda shorts and a bright tropical shirt crossed his legs and reached into the metal ice container for a bottle of champagne.

Remo made a short move toward the gray plug but the ruddy-faced gentleman lifted a finger indicating Remo had made a naughty. "Uh, uh. Remember the plug. You can't swim with lead weights, can you?"

Remo shook his head and sat back to listen. The man uncorked the champagne, brought out a champagne glass and rested it on the metal container. Then he popped the cork and poured the glass full.

Remo, who was trying to teach himself psychology, assumed that this was the acting out of a fantasy, sort of action-reaffirmation-of-an-event, to reinforce its reality. He liked that analysis, although he wasn't quite sure he understood his own words. He wished he could find someone to try them out on and if they didn't understand them either, he just might have gotten the whole thing right.

"Excuse the libation, if you will," said the ruddy-faced man who had introduced himself as Harry Magrudder, "but you see, it's a little reward I am allowing myself at the culmination of a year and a half's work." The man who called himself Harry Magrudder downed a glass, poured himself another, placed the champagne bottle on the metal shelf, sipped from the glass. The clear tropical sun glistened off the edge of the glass and made the champagne appear as if riddled with sunbeams.

"I'd offer you one, Mister whatever your last

23

name is. I believe it's Katner this week; one time it was Pelham, another time Green, another Willis and heaven knows what other names at other times. But I know you don't drink.

"And you don't smoke. You eat very little meat, —but a lot of fish. You often stay with an elderly Korean gentleman. Occasionally you have sex, which causes you some problems because the women seem to insist on more. Recently, you have taken to only going to bed with a woman the night before you leave a place. Is that correct?"

"No," Remo said. "That's absolutely not correct. You must have me confused with someone else."

"Perhaps I have you confused with the bodyguard for that Chinese general. You remember the little incident in Peking; rumors about an old Korean called the Master of Sinanju and his disciple, who was called Shiva, the Destroyer."

"I remember nothing," Remo said. "You've got to believe me, Mr. Magrudder. My name is Remo Katner and I'm a salesman for Sensitivity Laboratories in Ocean —City, Long Island. We sell success programs to corporations, universities, schools—for people to make better use of their potential. I'm a simple guy trying to make a buck. I went out to fish today and now you got me strapped in this thing."

"I'm sure you know a lot about human potential. Your's is rather interesting. Very interesting, as a matter of fact. So interesting that I knew I was a millionaire the second time you crossed my path."

The man who called himself Magrudder sipped again from the champagne and put the glass near the bottle. He folded his arms around his red, sunburned knees.

"I'm in the, shall we say, security business. I work for the government. Some thing very strange happened at a little think-tank outside of Washington some time back. It seems an ex-Nazi got killed in a chess game. A parachute instructor lost his chute on the way down. A gang of toughs was beaten up by one man, and just before that a former employee at the think-tank was found with his head in a paint-can shaker

—"My department was watching the think-tank carefully because the Russians were interested in it. Well, to make a long story short, we were told to drop the search for the security officer there who disappeared, a Remo Pelham. That was the first clue.

—"Then there was the China incident when our department was called off the disappearance of General Liu. Very interesting—because my department ordinarily would have prime responsibility.

"So, I and a few other people decided to check back further, especially when bodies—internationally related bodies—turned up very rapidly during that China incident. And there were other strange things. The sudden fortunate disappearance of the executioner of the Cosa Nostra in New York. Here one day. Gone the next. And we ran into the record of an old employee who killed himself in a hospital by tearing out tubes with his hook. You should know the name of the gentleman. His name was Conrad MacCleary."

The man who called himself Magrudder finished the glass and poured himself another, savoring the first sip.

"So I checked. And would you believe that this MacCleary was listed as working for us at that moment, and we had no record of what he was doing.

25

Oh, we had a record all right. It was false. It had him in Bangkok. And my department head said never mind, some secret presidential mission or something. Does this story interest you?"

"Sure, Mr. Magrudder, but I'd like it a lot more if I could listen to it outside of this contraption."

"I'm sure you would. That's why you're in it. I probably wouldn't even get a chance to finish my story. And I'm sure you'll want to hear how it's going to end. So I'm taking the wee liberty of the life jacket to make sure you hear me out."

"My life, Mr. Magrudder, is not a wee liberty. Please let me out of this. I've always been afraid of drowning."

The man who called himself Magrudder giggled slightly. "Good. You just stay afraid of me and we'll be fine."

"Now, follow me, if you will," he continued. "I and two other people I trust began keeping little notes. Nothing big at first, just notes of these strange occurrences and certain small events that seemed to go extremely well for the nation with no apparent reason. Luck, it was attributed to, I believe. And then, one day, my stroke of genius. I put myself in the place of a young president who was to be assassinated in Dallas.

"I said to myself, *you're the President and you've got a problem.*"

Magrudder finished the bottle by draining it into his mouth and tossed it overboard with a splash. He took out another one from the case and this time did not bother pouring into the champagne glass. He drank directly from the bottle.

"Excuse the indulgence," he said, "but a year-

and-a-half of sobriety must end with a certain joy. In any event, I said, I'm the President and I've got a problem. Crime is increasing. If I tell my police no holds are barred, we get a police state. If I don't, we get chaos, and then, if Machievelli's right, we get a police state anyway. I want to save the country. So what do I do?

"I figured what the President did. He decided to create an organization that didn't exist. It could break the law to enforce the law, but since it didn't exist, it would not endanger the Constitution.

"So I, the President, create this organization, and only I and maybe my vice president and two other men know about it. The man who runs it and the man who heads the killer-arm. The man who heads the killer-arm has to know, because he must violate the law and if he were captured and believed he worked for the FBI or the CIA or what-have-you, then it would be just as bad for the country if he confessed to that. You see, so he knows.

"And he knows that if he gets into trouble, all he has to do is say he works for the Mafia or something like that and his group will get him out. The head of that killer-arm is you, Remo whatever-your-name is. You see, that security guard who disappeared from the think-tank and the special guard for the Chinese general had identical fingerprints. And surprise, surprise—those fingerprints were not to be found in the FBI files, where the fingerprints of all law enforcement people reside."

"Mr. Magrudder, what do you want from me?"

The man called Magrudder giggled. "I'm glad you asked that. Two million dollars in cash and five hundred thousand dollars a year for the rest of my life. I know your people can pay it. An outfit like yours would spend more than that on a computer system."

"What makes you think I can get you the money?"

"Because, Remo, there are three envelopes with the whole story of facts and places; any one of them might wind up at the *New York Times* or the *Washington Post* if I should fail to do something each day at a set time. For your organization to be exposed is to fail. Goodbye to what little confidence remains in the government's ability to govern within the law. Goodbye Constitution. Goodbye America."

Magrudder laughed into his bottle of champagne as he lifted it and some spilled over his ruddy face and down his thick neck.

"You're full of crap, Mr. Magrudder. If you had all this information, you'd have more than three envelopes."

The man who called himself Magrudder raised a finger. "No way, my boy, *no way*. What if one should get out by accident? No. I needed enough to deter you people, but not so many as to precipitate an accident. Two would have been safer against accidents, but maybe you would have discovered one, leaving me only one envelope as a margin against death. That would be too thin. Four, however, would have been asking for trouble. So I picked three."

"Let's see," said Remo. "Your aunt Harriet in Cheyenne has one and you've got another and . . . the third. Who's got the third?"

The grin disappeared momentarily from the fat red face but then returned.

"One is as good as a hundred, my boy, and I'll ex-

28

tend that margin of safety when I get back to the hotel."

"You're so confident because you have four or five or ten of those envelopes stashed around," Remo said. "You don't have the kind of guts, Hopkins, to live one envelope away from death."

Harry Hopkins, the man called Magrudder, blinked. "So. You know my name. Well, well. Congratulations. But you don't know me, sonny boy. You skinny young punk. You've got to live one way if you're going to make it big. There are only three envelopes. Now row me back to the frigging hotel and call your boss. I want the down payment by tomorrow afternoon."

He swilled the champagne deeply and snorted his contempt. "Get a move on, skinny," he said. "The only reason I'm keeping you alive is you're my only contact with that organization."

Remo rubbed his hands together and sighed. "That's where you're wrong. I'm your second contact with the organization."

"Yeah? Who's the first?"

"The man who has the third envelope," Remo said and he smiled.

"Horseshit," Harry Hopkins said.

"Nope," said Remo sweetly. "Let me describe him to you. He's tight-lipped, obnoxious, vicious, ruthless and totally without human compassion for anything but his golf game. And at *that* he cheats. I beat him once even with his fourteen-pencil handicap and as much as he hated that, he hated my losing a golf ball more. He is cheap beyond belief. I mean cheap. I think that's why he was chosen."

"You're lying," screamed Harry Hopkins. "You're

29

lying. The man is absolutely trustworthy. We even wondered how he got into the business, he was so honest."

"I rang the bell with cheap, didn't I?" Remo asked.

"You're not getting any more information from me." Hopkins moved his foot to the gray plug, but stopped suddenly and his mouth dropped open. "No," he said.

"Yes," said Remo slipping the last clinging strap of the lead weighted life preserver off his arm. It had been a good set of locks but he could have cracked them if he wanted to. He didn't have to. The chain fasteners had been attached to a nylon band guaranteed to hold three hundred pounds of pressure. It was better than that. It had held close to four hundred.

"Want to pull the plug, sweetheart?" Remo said. "I rang the bell with cheap, huh?"

"I've known the man who has had the envelope for years. Years. He'd never betray a friend," Hopkins said. "He got out of the business because it was too dirty. He retired from it. He's been in on this from the beginning, giving me counsel and advice. And I trust him."

"Make believe you're the President, Hopkins. Who else would you put in charge of such an operation?"

Remo stood up in the bow of the boat and went to the seat near the gray plug. He looked down at the perspiring red-faced man beneath him.

Hopkins looked up, in panic, then slowly shrugged. "Mind if I have another drink?"

"Sure," Remo said. "Your being an alcoholic is going to be the cover for your death anyway."

"I'm not an alcoholic and you'll kill me if I take

30

another drink or not. So. Bottoms up." Remo saw the bottom of the bottle come up; the reddish eyelids close and air-bubbles rise from within the neck of the bottle.

"Okay, so you're not an alcoholic," Remo said.

"I haven't had a drink for a year and a half until today." He lowered the bottle between his legs. "Tell me," he said, "how come I couldn't find fingerprints on you anywhere? I mean how did you people hide that?"

"Simple," Remo said. "I'm a dead man. Remo Williams. Name mean anything to you?"

"Doesn't ring a bell." The bottle went up again.

"Policeman executed for a killing in Newark?"

The fat man shook his head. "You really dead?" he asked.

"You might say so. Yeah. It's a good way not to exist."

"Couldn't think of a better one," Hopkins said. "Say why don't you let me live until at least I get you guys my notes? What if someone finds my notes and the carbons of the letters?"

"Sorry, pal. There are no notes and no carbons. Only three letters. One I took out of your room. Your aunt Harriet had the second and she lost that one today when she was involved in a terrible accident. The third is with Dr. Harold W. Smith. Your friend. My boss. The head of CURE. You're out of the game"

"Can I have another bottle? One more. I mean a last drink. Okay?"

Remo reached into the metal container, felt through the ice for another bottle, grabbed it by the neck and hoisted it out as Hopkins made a lunge for

31

his groin. Hopkins found himself suddenly seated right back where he was, with a bottle in his hand. He opened it, tried to catch Remo's head with the cork, missed, shrugged and said, "You'd kill me anyway, drink or no drink. You know I could nurse this if I wanted to." He drank deeply. "I'm no alcoholic."

"If you say so," Remo said.

It was a beautiful cove he saw, rising dark and green from the clear sweet Caribbean. A paradise. Some people went to this place for their honeymoon and brought their families back later. People who could get married and reproduce their kind.

"Say, you know I was thinking," Hopkins said. "Why don't you bring me into CURE. I'm pretty smart. I figured out something was going on. Now you know you could get me anytime, right? You can use a good brain. Look, I'm no alky no matter what anyone tells you. Ask Smith. Well, don't ask him 'cause he thinks anyone who takes two drinks is an alcoholic. But I'd be good. I would. Real good."

Remo's mouth became dry and his stomach felt the slow dissolution of distaste. He did not look down at the man beneath him, but out to the flatness of the sea until it curved round in the distance. People now knew the world was round. And this proved it. It was simple. It's always simple after someone else does it for you. Hopkins was still talking.

"Okay, I understand why Smith might not want me. But if you control the killer-arm. . . ."

"I am the killer-arm."

"Well, if you're the killer-arm, boy, could you hold up CURE. Huh? What about it? Huh? Like the idea, don't you?"

"It's great. Finish your drink."

"A deal? Huh? A deal?"

"No," said Remo.

"Ah, you're probably just some low-rank gunman. There's gotta be more than one guy in the killer-arm. About as much chance of you being it as me being an alcoholic. Last drink. The last one."

Remo looked down at the man who looked at his last drink.

"I could take this or leave this, you know. I'm not an alcoholic. Take it or leave it. But I'm gonna take it because you're going to kill me anyway. Bottoms up."

When Remo saw the last air bubble stop in the bottle as the last of the champagne drained into Hopkins' open gullet, he pushed with his right knee, sending the man leftward and with his right hand he reached out, grabbed the fat rolled neck and pushed, out and down into the tepid blue-green water of the Caribbean where he gently drowned the thrashing figure.

If anyone hidden in the cove had been watching, it would have appeared that Hopkins fell over the side and Remo reached for him but it was too late. Even though Remo reached into the water all the way up to his armpit, he was unable to reach him, and was able to grab him into the boat only three minutes later when the man floated up. But it was too late. He was dead. Well, the coroner said, every alcoholic drinks himself into the grave if he thinks he's not an alcoholic. "They just can't take a single drink, can they, sir?"

CHAPTER THREE

For Westerners who get hanged, or shot, or cut to death or freeze in passes that are unpassable in winter, there are mournful ballads sung from generation to generation.

For Vinnie the Rock Palumbo, there wasn't even a missing persons report by his wife. When you are married to a Vincent Alphonse Palumbo and he does not return from a "sweet little job" you do not wish law enforcement people to know about it. Because then you, too, may not return from a walk to the supermarket or a visit to relatives.

If you are Vinnie Palumbo's father you do not miss him all that much, because the last time you saw him was eighteen years ago, when he took a pipe to your skull over an allowance dispute.

If you are Willie the Plumber Palumbo, you definitely do not talk about your brother's disappearance, because you have a very good idea what happened to him.

And if you are Vinnie the Rock Palumbo, you make no noise to anyone because you are frozen inside the cab of your Ocean Wheel tractor trailer truck, your body like rock, your eyes ice crystals in your white frosted skull.

It indeed had been a sweet job. Your brother had said: "It's a fast two hundred dollars to drive a truck a couple of blocks."

And you answered: "You're full of crap, Willie the Plumber. How much of it are you taking a walk with?"

"Okay, Vinnie," Willie the Plumber had said, coughing through his cigarette. "Because you're my brother, three hundred dollars."

"Five hundred."

"Five hundred. That's what I'm getting to pay you."

"Five hundred in advance."

"A hundred in advance and four hundred later. Okay? You got your teamsters' card?"

"I got my teamsters' card. And I ain't moving, until I get three hundred dollars up front."

"Okay. Because you're my brother, two hundred fifty dollars up front and for anyone else I'd say no."

So you, Vincent the Rock Palumbo, drive your rig onto Pier 27 one hot August morning and by 4 p.m., the Ocean Wheel container was hooked onto your horse and you drive slowly out. You also notice that people in cars are closing in on you for a tail and a hot dog truck starts to move out.

You notice three squad cars of local bulls in plain-clothes, but you keep a steady pace, and getting no signals from the car in front of you in which your brother sits, you follow it to a warehouse where your truck gets a new paste-on sign calling it Chelsea Trucking. Apparently you suddenly are no longer being tailed.

You wait until dark, then pull out again with the three other trucks following, and this time you are

35

following somebody else, not your brother, in a car ahead. You follow him to the entrance of the New Jersey Turnpike where he signals you to take a cutoff to the new Hudson Industrial Park complex; two buildings and a set of swamps. You are instructed to drive your truck down a ramp into a hole in the ground and wait. You had been told not to pack any weapons, so you brought two. A .38 special in the glove compartment and a .45 under the seat.

You expertly park your rig in the right hand corner of the square pit with the metal and tubular linings. The other men maneuver their vehicles next to yours so that you are part of four trucks side by side in the same metal lined pit. You are told to stay in your trucks.

You take out your .45, just in case. You see the driver next to you reach for something also. Behind you, heavy steel doors close off the ramp. Overhead, a roof comes down over the trucks in the pit, in prefabricated sections. You were told to stay where you were, so you do, but get out of your cab to chat with the driver next to you. He tells you he is getting six hundred dollars for the drive. You curse your sonofabitch brother, Willie the Plumber Palumbo.

It is dark; there are no lights. Soon the matches wear out. One of the men has a flashlight. You search your cab. No flashlight. For a few blocks, you certainly weren't going to buy one and the truck owners did not provide one.

The driver next to you suggests you open one of the trucks, maybe it's liquor that was hijacked. You say no because the people will be back in a minute and for a ten dollar bottle of booze who the hell wants to blow a few hundred bucks.

The driver next to you says booze would be good now because it's getting chilly in this place. You are dressed for the summer and indeed it is getting chilly. One of the drivers on the other side is banging the sealed section where the ramp was. He is yelling to be let out. Suddenly, you go weak. What if they aren't going to let you out?

That's impossible. You've got the goods. Besides, you've got artillery to enforce it. If they want the goods, they've got to come back.

You start stamping your feet and banging your ribs. You're in a damn freezer. When you get hold of Willie, you're going to mess him up good.

One of the guys says they should shoot their way out and someone further over says this is stupid because they're not only underground but those are freezing coils and if you rupture one of those, you'll be gassed.

So you climb into your cab and start your engine and turn on the heater until you hear a knocking at the window. It's one of the drivers. He says to save everyone from carbon monoxide poisoning, they should all get in one cab and use just one heater.

You say okay and they all pile into yours, four guys crammed into the cab. One of them starts praying. About 6 a.m. by the watch, the truck is running out of diesel fuel so one of the guys says he will go to get more from the other trucks. He doesn't come back. It gets colder in the cab even with the bodies and it's hard to breathe. You draw matches for who is to go to one of the other trucks for fuel. You curse yourself for not taking the fuel at the beginning, but then no one expected to be in there that long. The guy who had parked next to you draws short. You all

37

chip in your shirts, so that he is wearing three summer shirts.

When you open the cab door, you know he is not going to make it, because you can practically cut the carbon monoxide fumes. You turn off the lights because with the engine down, you need the battery as much as possible.

You're alone with one other driver and about noon, shivering shirtless in the cab, he asks you to shoot him. You say no because you have enough sins on your soul already. He begs. He says he'll do it himself if you don't.

You don't and he starts to cry and the tears freeze on his face. You're not feeling anything. If you don't kill yourself and offer this up to God, maybe he'll take you into heaven, or, at least, purgatory. You had always planned to make amends and you vow that if you get out, you're going straight.

And then you are numb all over. You're very sleepy and you wonder why you had always feared death.

Thus ended the ballad of Vinnie the Rock Palumbo.

      Oh, Frozen to Death.
      Oh, Frozen to Death.
      On a hot August Day in New Jersey.

CHAPTER FOUR

The frail wisp of an aged oriental was named Chiun and Remo Williams watched him with respect.

Chiun stood on top of a chest of drawers near a porthole in the stateroom, a spiral bound notebook in his hand.

He tore out one sheet of paper, then held it at arm's length like a dirty diaper, out over the floor.

He opened his fingers and released the paper and softly said, "go."

The paper fluttered down, sloshing from side to side. When it was four feet from the floor, it stopped, speared on Remo's fingertips.

Remo pulled the torn paper off his fingertips and won a smile from Chiun. "Good," the old Oriental said, the smiling creasing the parchment texture of his face. "Now again."

This time Chiun crumpled the paper slightly and reached up on tiptoes before letting it drop and calling "go." The paper dropped faster, with less side-to-side movement. It dropped straight to the floor and lay there on the nylon carpet like an unanswered accusation.

Chiun stared angrily at Remo. "Why?" he said.

Remo was laughing. "I can't help it, Chiun. You look so damn silly standing up there. I was thinking you'd look terrific if I had you sprayed gold and put you on my mantel. Then I had to laugh. People do, you know."

"I am well aware," Chiun said in his clipped, precise Oriental tones, "that mankind is the only species that laughs. Mankind is also the only species that dies from lack of conditioning. It may happen to you, Remo, if you do not practice. This floater stroke is very important and very useful, but it must be done correctly."

And for the twentieth time on the cruise aboard the S. S. Atlantica, Remo heard the explanation of the floater stroke. How it depended for its effectiveness on the mass of the victim or the object to be struck. That there was no energy loss between the time the stroke was uncocked and impact. But that if the object were missed, the force could easily dislocate the striker's shoulder.

"Chiun," Remo had said, "I know seventy-eight different strokes. I know strokes with the finger and the toes, with the hands, knuckles, feet, elbows, and knees and even with my hipbones. What the hell do I need another one for?"

"Because you must be perfect. After all, are you not Shiva, the Destroyer?" and Chiun had cackled, as he had so often since they had returned from China on a mission for the President during which Remo was thought to be the reincarnation of one of the Hindu gods. Chiun chuckled about it only when he talked to Remo. He laughed to no one else, for a very simple reason. He believed the story. Remo Williams was Shiva the Destroyer.

But he was also Chiun's pupil and now Chiun tore another piece of paper from the notebook, held it above his head, released it, and softly called, "go."

The paper fluttered down gently, and then it was not one sheet of paper anymore, it was two, sliced in half lengthwise by a chop from the hand of Remo Williams.

It would have been a very impressive display if anyone had seen it. But their suite of cabins was on the very top deck of the Atlantica. Outside their glass door and porthole windows, the deck had been sealed off as a private verandah, and there was only the sea.

Below the deck their cabins were on was another deck and below that another deck, and then another and another, until you were down in the bowels of the ship, and there were no more portholes because you were right at the waterline. There were cabins down there too except the furniture was not walnut, it was chipped paint steel and the floors had no carpet, they had only linoleum tile. And in the stern of the ship, in the cheapest, rockiest cabin the Atlantica had to offer, was Dr. Harold W. Smith, head of CURE, one of the several most powerful men in the world.

He lay in his hard bed trying desperately to focus his eyes on a spot in the ceiling until his stomach returned to normal. He had a theory that if he could somehow lock his eyes onto the spot, and then move when the spot moved, it would reduce the feeling of motion and he might survive.

But down that deep in a ship, the motion is not only one of rocking. The ship slides from side to side as well. It slid then and the spot went port. Dr. Smith went starboard and he kept going starboard until he rolled over onto his stomach and was reaching desperately for the waste paper basket.

Damn that Remo Williams. Sometimes Dr. Smith

wondered if winning the war against crime was really worth having to put up with him.

Dr. Smith had contacted Remo in Nassau, where his cruise ship had tied up, and told Remo he should fly back to the states immediately for reassignment. Remo had refused. He told Dr. Smith he had made the finals of the dancing contest on board the ship and so he would have to cruise back or miss his chance at the gold cup. Why didn't Dr. Smith fly down and sail back with him, Remo suggested.

"We'll have plenty of time then to talk about the new assignment," Remo said.

"I don't have the time to go sailing around the world with you," Smith had said.

"Then I won't tell you what happened to your old buddy Hopkins and his plan to blackmail CURE. You'll find out about it someday when you get a secret letter in the mail asking you for forty-three billion dollars in ones."

"Very funny," Smith said. "I know what happened to Hopkins. I got a report."

"Oh, balls. Well, come on down anyway and I'll tell you what I did to Howard Hughes," Remo said. He had insisted and importuned and become stubborn, and finally, after he guaranteed that he would get Smith a good cabin, Smith had agreed.

And now here he was, vomiting up his youth and his future, and hating Remo Williams more each minute.

But Harold W. Smith had not gotten where he was by shirking duty. He had not been tapped to head CURE, the government's secret crime-fighting agency, because he lacked character. So he slowly got to his feet and, staggering slightly, moved across the room to take a black suitcase out of his closet. It was made of cardboard and it had no travel stickers on it. Then, carefully locking his door behind him, he began the walk up five decks to Remo Williams' suite of cabins.

It was after 3 a.m. and the ship had gone to sleep. He met no one on the stairs or in the corridors. But Remo Williams was not in his room.

The decks were more deserted than the corridors now. It was wet and raw out on the decks and the wind swirled knifingly up out of the sea, impelling a fine mist across the ship and chilling the bones of anyone who stood there.

But Remo Williams was not cold. He looked carefully around the small wall that fenced off his private section of deck from the rest of the ship. There was no one in sight, which was as it should be.

Under his hands, Remo felt the heavy oaken top of the deck rail. It was five inches across, curved and wet from the mist of the sea. Remo kicked off his canvas slippers and hopped up unto the rail. He stood there for a moment, balanced precariously, standing straight up, seventy-five feet above the water, as he absorbed the ocean's roll into his senses and let the muscles of his legs and nerves of his bare feet catch the hard rocking rhythms of the ship's movement. Then he began to run, out around his verandah wall; then down the ship, balanced along the top of the deck railing. The ship rocked and rolled and slipped from side to side, but Remo ran rapidly in a world of his own.

He ran a few steps straight forward, one leg after another, his bare feet so quickly removed from the wet polished railing that they had no time to slip.

43

And then in full motion, he would turn his body until he was skittering sideways, one leg crossing over in front of the other, then behind. As he ran, he looked out at the sea and he realized why sailors had a special arrogance, because here, away from land, in the middle of an ink-cold sea, man challenged God, and only the arrogant could achieve victory.

Remo had now reached the stern of the ship and he slowed to make sure no one had ventured out onto the deck. When he saw it was clear, he picked up his speed and continued racing around the oak railing, making the turn and heading back up toward the bow as fast as he could move. He glanced below him into the glass-enclosed swimming pool.

Ordinarily, a burly man with a mustache would have been sitting there. He was a fire chief from the Midwest, filled with loud opinions and ignorance, and he had sat there almost all day and all night on the trip down. He had called Chiun a "chink" when he thought the old man could not hear, but Remo had heard. Later Remo had seen him pick up a tip that someone had left on a waiter's tray, and so, when it became necessary to clear out a cabin to make room for Harold W. Smith, Remo had his candidate.

The Midwestern fire chief one fine day on the beach of Paradise Island, had mysteriously fallen asleep. He had slept in the hot summer sun for four hours and when he was awakened, the skin was already blistering. At Nassau General Hospital, they treated him for sun poisoning and severe burns, and cautioned him about staying out in the sun too long, then decided to hold him for treatment and observation, after he said that he had been knocked out by a

44

touch on the shoulder from a husky young man with deep brown eyes.

Remo grinned as he passed over the empty chair and thought to himself that if the fire chief was a bad tipper, Smith was even worse. The waiters had gained nothing on the switch.

Remo padded silently across one of the steel cross-beams that held up the curved plastic roof of the swimming pool, then was back on the port side of the ship. He ran a few more steps, glided quickly around the barrier separating the public deck from his private verandah, and landed noiselessly on the deck outside his cabin.

He slid his feet back into his slippers and walked into the cabin through the sliding glass door.

Smith was sitting on the sofa and Chiun was kneeling behind him, pressing practiced fingers into clumps of nerves along the sides of Smith's neck.

"Thank you, Chiun," Smith said, pulling away as Remo came in.

"Seasick, huh?," Remo said.

"Never. I've spent more time at sea then you've spent sober," Smith sniffed. "Out for your evening stroll?"

"You might say that," Remo said, and then because he wanted to be cruel to this man who brought him dehumanizing missions and assignments, he said: "Hopkins knew it was you right away. As soon as I said cheap, he knew."

"Yes, yes. Well, that will do," Smith said. He rolled his eyes toward Chiun, who despite his deadly skills and despite his love for Remo did not really know what CURE was or what it did, and was content to know only that Remo was sent on killing missions and that it was his job to see that Remo was adequate to the task.

Chiun had sunk back on the sofa, slipping easily into a lotus position and closing his eyes. Smith stood up and opened his suitcase. He reached inside and brought out a shiny paper packet and held it toward Remo.

"Do you know what this is?"

"Sure, it's a fix. Heroin," Remo said, taking the packet in his hands.

"Do you know people would kill me for it?"

"Sweetheart, there are people who would kill you just for the fun of it," Remo said.

"Be serious, will you?" Smith said.

Ignoring Remo's faint protestation that he was being serious, Smith went on: "That's our problem right now. "Every year, illegal narcotics peddlers in the United States sell maybe eight tons of heroin. Most of the traffic's controlled by the Mafia. They grow the poppies in Turkey, process them in France or South America and smuggle them into the country. The Treasury Department slows them down. It harrasses them. Occasionally, it makes a big arrest. But a big arrest is a suitcase full, maybe fifty pounds. And in the entire country, we use maybe sixteen thousand pounds a year. On the street, that's worth over a billion and a half dollars."

"So? Hire more men for the Treasury Department," Remo said.

"We tried that. It was all set up. And the Treasury men were killed. The stuff got in, Remo. We're not talking about suitcases full. We're talking about four truck loads. Maybe fifty tons. Enough heroin to supply the illegal market for six years. Ten billion dollars worth of heroin!

— "And when the Mafia forces out the small dealers," Smith said, "it might be worth twice that much."

Remo looked again at the glassine envelope in his hand and then tossed it back into Smith's open suitcase.

"What do you want me to do?," he shrugged.

"You know where Hudson, New Jersey, is, don't you? You're from that neighborhood, aren't you?," Smith asked.

— "I'm from Newark. Newark makes Hudson look like Beverly Hills," Remo said.

"Well, the heroin's in Hudson somewhere. It was unloaded from a ship there. Treasury people were killed following the trucks that were carrying it. And now the trucks are someplace in the city with the heroin and we can't find them."

"How do you know they're still there? They could be in Pittsburgh, you know."

"The trucks are still in Hudson. We've been monitoring every vehicle that leaves the city for the last week. A special tuber detector developed by the agriculture department. One of our guys adapted it and now it works as a heroin sensor too. Nothing big has left the city."

"I never heard of a gadget like that," Remo said.

— "Neither has our government. We've kept it secret. If we let them know about it, two weeks later the damn plans for it will be in *Scientific American* and the Mafia will have a defense for it, before we even get a chance to use it."

"Then why don't you just wait until your silly-ass tuber detector finds it?," Remo said.

47

"Because if we give them time, they can take it out by the cupful and we'll never be able to track it down. We want to find it before it gets into circulation in bits and pieces."

"Okay," Remo said, "who do you want me to hit?"

"I don't know. Maybe nobody."

"This isn't another one of those information things, is it?," Remo asked. "Every time I get involved in one of them, I nearly get killed."

"Not information," Smith said. "I want you to go in and start making noise. Get whoever's got the drugs to come after you. Then find out where the heroin is and destroy it. And if anybody gets in your way, destroy them. Destroy the whole damned city if you have to."

Remo had not seen Smith so worked up since the last time Remo had filed an expense voucher.

Smith went to the suitcase again. He took out a photograph. "This is an addict, Remo. This is what those bastards do to them."

Remo took the picture. It was a naked girl, maybe in her teens. But her eyes were blank and pained-looking, and her skin was swollen, ulcerated and black. In the upper-right-hand corner of the photo was a closeup inset of her arms and there was not a clear spot left in which a hypodermic syringe could be inserted.

"That girl's dead now," Smith said. "Some of them aren't so lucky."

He took the photograph back and put it back into his suitcase. He started talking again, calmer now. "Hudson's the chief port of entry. We have to think there's significant political leverage being used there to protect the heroin imports. The cops are crooked.

The politicians are crooked. The Mafia runs the town. But it's tight and we don't know much. The leader is a name named Verillio, we think. Or Gasso. Or Palumbo. We just don't know."

"What would be my cover?"

"You're Remo Barry. You've got an apartment with Chiun in New York. You're a staff writer for *Intelligentsia Annual*. Don't worry about it, we just bought the magazine. It was the cheapest one we could get. Go in as a journalist and poke around."

"Suppose I turn down the assignment?" Remo asked.

"Remo, please," Smith said. It was the first time in all the years that Smith had ever said please to him.

Remo just nodded. Smith reached again into the suitcase and pulled out a thick typewritten report. "All the data's in here, all the facts, all the names. Look it over. Memorize it. Then throw it away. You have a free hand to do whatever you want. Please, just do it fast."

It was the second please, and Remo did not try to think of anything smart-ass to say. He nodded again and Smith closed the suitcase and walked toward the door. Without a word, he left. He was glad he had not found it necessary to tell Remo that one of the addicts not yet lucky enough to be dead was Smith's own daughter.

CHAPTER FIVE

For Dominic Verillio, the good Italian restaurants would not do. Neither would his sprawling estate in Kensico, New York, nor his three-story English tudor home in Hudson, New Jersey. The Palm Beach home was out too. They were all being watched. Or bugged. Little electronic devices that so fitted the character of America. Neat. Clean. Technical. Unemotional. And you didn't know they didn't work until it was too late.

But they worked well enough so that Dominic Verillio would not even discuss big business in his office. Not well enough to stop him or even hinder him once he knew about them. But enough so the good restaurants, his country estate, his three-story home or his Palm Beach home were out for something that was really important. The flaw in electronic surveillance — was timing. Given time, the feds, the state police— even your credit agency—could bug any place you could build or buy or rent. Given time.

But what if you didn't give time? If you conducted your real business within ten minutes at a new location, you were as safe as if the bug had never been invented.

50

So on that bright afternoon when the center-lane trees on Park Avenue and 81st Street in New York City still gloried in their summer green, taxis began arriving on the east side of the street, pulling up one after another, letting off their passengers who were, invariably, one middle aged man accompanied by two young men. All between 2:05 p.m. and 2:10 p.m. The little crowd was consumed by bowing and hand-kissing and nodding until Dominic Verillio, in black business suit, white shirt and black tie, said:

"None of that. Not now. Not now."

And since most of the hand-kissing and bowing was to him, that stopped it. Five rented limousines pulled up, rented ten minutes before in five different locations and the group of people rapidly filled them.

Dominic Verillio was in the front limousine. It was the car of honor and therefore, with him also was Pietro Scubisci, a sweet-looking gray haired man from New York City in an off-the-rack suit and white shirt with upturned collar because his wife, now being seventy-two years of age, did not see so well as she used to.

Pietro Scubisci was *Capo Mafioso* in New York City and within a day and a half could present, if he wished, eighty-two million dollars, in cash in paper bags. The rolled up, crinkled brown paper bag he now held in his lap, however, contained fried peppers, in case Dominic Verillio was to hold the meeting in a restaurant. Scubisci did not like paying New York City restaurant prices because "all the time they go up." That he was in a degree responsible for this was not at issue. That was money coming in. Paying

51

the prices was money going out. He brought ~~his~~ peppers.

Beside him in the back seat was Francisco Salvatore, younger than Scubisci, in his early forties, in a Pierre Cardin suit whose stylish, flowing lines seemed incapable of wrinkling. He had sculptured hair, manicured fingernails, and a deep, tanned face. His teeth were white, even and flawless, and he was often told he could be a movie actor if he wished. He did not wish, however, because, at his age, making what Rock Hudson or John Wayne made would have been a pay cut.

He carried no money, because even cash would have altered the lines of his suit. When the elderly Scubisci turned to speak to him, he accidentally brushed the greasy bag against the knitted fabric of Salvatore's pants. If left a dark splotch. Salvatore pretended he did not notice it. Later, on the flight back to Los Angeles, he would curse silently to himself until the suit was off him and in the garbage pail.

To Scubisci's right was Filemeno Palmucci—or Fat O'Brien—a lump of a head set on a roll of a neck and expanding out from there to hips. The mound was topped by a gray fedora, a half-size too small. Fat O'Brien never smiled and just stared straight ahead, as if intent on digesting his intestines. He was from Boston.

In front, of course, was Don Dominic Verillio who had called them all together. He was half-turned, facing the back seat, and was polite and cordial. His face could have graced the cover of BUSINESS MANAGEMENT, but he spoke with more emotion and with gestures—more human as opposed to the cadaverlike expressions of top level American management.

"I take it you are in good health," said Dominic Verillio, smiling.

"Good," said Pietro Scubisci who had the right to answer first. "The wife she good too, although she no see too good now."

"I am sorry to hear that, Pietro."

"Life is life, Don Dominic," said Scubisci. "It begin blind and weak and end blind and weak. I did not make life."

"You would have made it better, Don Pietro," said Francisco Salvatore in a display of white teeth.

"Francisco. God make life. Nobody make it better. Nobody make it worse either," said Pietro Scubisci. Somehow the grease from his fried peppers never seemed to smudge his dark suit.

"And you?" said Verillio to Francisco Salvatore.

"I am well, thank you, Don Dominic. My wife is well. My children are well. It is a good life in the sunshine. You must visit us some time."

"I shall," said Dominic Verillio. "I shall."

"I'm fine too, Don Dominic," said Fat O'Brien.

"That is good. Health is most important. We have been having good weather here in the metropolitan area of New York. Good weather makes good wine, as they say."

"Good wine makes good weather, too," said Pietro Scubisci and smiled. All smiled with him.

And thus it went in the caravan of rented limousines. Health, weather, the family. The big innovative discussion came when Guglielmo Marconne, or Apples Donnelly as he was known from time to time, told Vittorio Pallellio that "you can't get a good steak in Miami Beach." They were in the fourth car from the front. Guglielmo Marconne was from Duluth and Vittorio Pallellio was from Miami Beach.

"We got good steaks," said Vittorio Pallellio. "Maybe you didn't look in the right places."

"I looked in the right places, Don Vittorio."

"You didn't look in the right places, Guglielmo."

"I looked in the Boca Del Sol."

"The Boca Del Sol doesn't have good steaks."

"I looked in—what's the name of that place that looks like a shlock furniture store?"

"That's the whole city, Guglielmo."

"I didn't get a good steak there, either. And I didn't get a good one in the Boca Del Sol."

"The Boca Del Sol doesn't have good steaks, Guglielmo."

"I know that. I got a bad steak there."

And so the small talk went among the representatives from Dallas and New Orleans, Chicago and Rochester, Portland and Kansas City, Cleveland and Columbus, Cincinnati, Louisville, Denver, Phoenix, Norfolk, Charleston, Las Vegas, San Francisco, Philadelphia and Wheeling.

Downtown went the caravan which, because the rented limousines were not all the same color, did not look like a caravan. Only Don Dominic Verillio knew the destination and every so often he would tell the driver to turn here and turn there, always careful not to lose the cars behind. Finally, before a small art shop in Greenwich Village, Don Dominic Verillio signaled his driver to stop.

He jumped out, opening the door for Pietro Scubisci, Francisco Salvatore and Fat O'Brien, saying "no time for formalities. No time."

The driver, Willie the Plumber Palumbo, also

jumped out and, checking a wad of bills in his pocket, ran into the little boutique art store with the dresses and paintings in front.

Almost as soon as he opened the door, he said, "There is a strawberry scene here I want to buy for $5,000."

"Into the back room," Don Dominic Verillio told his guests. "Just go into the back."

To each car that stopped, he said, "The back room. The back room."

Within forty-five seconds, he was following the last man into the art shop, the sign above which read "Eve Flynn."

The attractive owner was still talking to Willie the Plumber. "Oh, my dear," she said. "So many people at once. This is wonderful. I always knew it would happen like this."

Her flaming red hair bounced as she threw back her head and rammed a hand on an outstretched hip, clad in paint-splattered blue jeans.

"This pitcher here by the door," said Willie the Plumber. "Right here. Dis one. Here is the money. But first I wanna know watcher modi . . . modi . . . what's the word, moderation is."

"Motivation," said the woman.

"Yeah. What dat is and how you tink of ya'self in de relativition of let's say Goggin."

"Gaugin?"

"Yeah. Him."

"I'm glad you asked," said the woman, her head jerking nervously to the mob that had just passed her headed to her back room where her Paris street scenes were. "But don't you think I should help them?"

"No," said the driver. "They're just looking. I want dis here pitcher and yer gonna take care of me."

"Certainly. You know I have a confession. You're my first customers. All so sudden." She pointed toward the back. "Are they bankers?"

"Dey're da American Kiwanis International."

"Funny. I didn't think so. They seemed too polite for that. Well, now you see, Gaugin saw life, Gaugin saw color differently. . . ." and the red headed artist was off into her explanation of color as an art form, as Willie the Plumber nodded and went over his four more questions mentally. He would use them if she slowed up. He would not have to use them.

In the back room, Don Dominic Verillio raised his hands, both for silence and as an indication that the formalities of gathering should be abandoned. He stood before a dark green-blue impression of a night park.

"Last year, I told you all individually when I visited you that drugs had become a serious problem. I told you that little independent dealers all over America were importing and selling heroin. Many of your people were involved. Many of your people were more involved in heroin than in working for you. Many of your own people were losing respect for you because they could independent the merchandise at a better price.

"What could you buy? A suitcase of the stuff. None of you ever got a trunk-full. Quality was irregular. People were selling you sugar. Sand. Baking powder. Cutting the stuff with strychnine. When you got pure stuff, people began overdosing. To get money for their habits, the junkies robbed indiscriminately. More crime. More police. More police meant you had to provide bigger pads and that was only when you could get them to take *mordido,* payoffs. This heroin stuff is going to kill us as sure as if we were shooting it up ourselves."

Grunts of agreement filled the room. A few men looked nervously out the door. They were within earshot of the shop's proprietor.

"Don't worry about her," said Don Dominic.

"She can hear," said Fat O'Brien.

"She's in her own world. An artist that good has a high of a different kind. We're here to talk horse. When I talked to you last year about my plans in your supposedly safe offices and homes, it took less than a week before it was known where we didn't want it known. Now I told you I was going to bring in tons of the stuff. You expressed doubts. Well, I'm ready to take orders."

"You mean, it's really coming in?" said Francisco Salvatore.

"It *is* in," said Don Dominic Verillio. "Forty seven tons. It's 98 per cent pure and we're going to ship it in pills that the junkies can break down and in serum bottles that look like they could be medicine. We're gonna be able to sell this stuff so cheap they'll be able to smoke it, like in Vietnam.

"You're going to be able to take the bottom out of this market and when you've cleaned out the independents, you can raise the ceiling on it. You'll own whole cities. I mean, *own* them. America can say goodbye to the glassine envelope."

"Don Dominic. Don Dominic. Don Dominic," the *capos* cried. Pietro Scubisci kissed the hand of Dominic Verillio, but Don Dominic knew that was more of an opener to bargain for bulk-rates rather than a sign of respect.

"And none of you knew it, did you? Forty-seven tons and none of you knew it. Now tell me who to worry about listening in and who not to worry about. Tell me what a safe place is and what a safe place isn't. I will take your orders now, once, and we will meet again in six months for more orders. The same way."

"You must have the fix in big," said Pietro Scubisci, who was the first to order.

"I got the best fix you can get. They don't come any better," Don Dominic said.

And Scubisci ordered a ton for New York City. Seven hundred pounds were destined for Los Angeles, 200 pounds for Boston, 600 pounds for Detroit, 300 pounds for Dallas and another 300 for New Orleans, 700 pounds for Philadelphia and a ton for Chicago. Cleveland wanted 300 pounds and Columbus 100 and Cincinnati 100. San Francisco ordered 200 pounds as did Kansas City. Fifty pounds each were ordered by Denver, Phoenix, Norfolk and Raleigh, and Charleston, Las Vegas, and Wheeling.

Don Dominic Verillio totaled it up mentally. Over eight thousand pounds, more than four tons. It was about a six-months' supply for the entire nation. He was satisfied. Orders would grow in size as he proved ability to deliver.

"We'll get it to you," he said. "And it'll have labels of your local druggists. You won't be able to tell the stuff from aspirin, penicillin or seidlitz powder. Gentlemen, this is the big fix." He smiled as befits a man who has just sold $160 million worth of goods to men who would resell them for $800 million.

"Don Dominic, Don Dominic, Don Dominic," again came the voices and Don Dominic Verillio received the adulation. He stood at the doorway and said goodbye to each one personally, as they went out to the front of the shop and then out to the street where the cars waited. The artist hardly looked up.

Scubisci was the last to leave.

"Pietro," said Don Dominic. "I have loved you like a father. I give you, with utmost respect, some advice."

"The Scubisci family always welcomes the advice of Don Dominic Verillio."

"As I told the others, if you don't sell high at first, you can establish your control. I say this for your own good."

"That is good advice if there is a second shipment."

"Is there something that makes you believe there won't be?"

"I am an old man, Don Dominic. Who knows if I live to a second shipment?"

"That is not what worries you," Verillio said.

"If I tell you what causes me concern, you laugh. As I laugh. I think it not worth your ears."

"Anything you say is worth my ears."

The old man nodded slowly. "My Angela, she believe in the stars. The stars this—the stars that. She plays her games. I listen. You know how she said you gonna get married. And you did. And how your wife die. And, may I bless her memory, she did. You know how she says you be *capo* of all *capos*. And you are. Maybe it an accident. She also say you get fine daughter and you no have children, so you knows what the stars say?"

Don Dominic's grip tightened on the old man's
59

shoulders. But as soon as it tightened, he caught control of himself and loosened.

"Well," continued Pietro Scubisci, rolling his greasy pepper bag in his fingers. "She come up a crazy this time. I tell you last year, this thing maybe is not the best thing. But I go along."

"Yes?" said Verillio.

"You know how Angela say this day is not the day and to wait and she says wait forever, so you don't wait at all. But I go along because stars are stars and business is business. But this time Angela is frightened. She say . . . you must promise no laugh. She say you going against a god."

Don Dominic could not control the laughter, and he apologized as he guffawed.

"You see, it is nothing," said Pietro.

"Tell me about this god."

"Well, it's not like a god, like a saint. It's like olden times God."

"Zeus. Jupiter. Apollo?"

"Like Chinese," Scubisci said. "A crazy thing. Angela sends away to this old lady in Greenwich Village, because the stars Angela cannot read. And comes back more confusion. What is the word the Jews use when they mourn their dead. Sit on boxes and do not shave and things?"

"*Shiva*," Verillio said.

"Yah. That's him. Except it sounds like sleeve."

"Shiva? Well, I'll be on the lookout for any eastern gods," Verillio said.

Pietro Scubisci smiled and shrugged. "I tell you it crazy. It's just that sometimes Angela. . . ." and his voice tailed off as the two men left the shop together and Willie the Plumber made his five thousand dollar purchase.

That night, Don Dominic Verillio made a mental note to look up the god, Shiva, in an encyclopedia.

CHAPTER SIX

Remo Williams waited in the sedate outer office of Dominic Verillio, chairman of the Hudson Action Council, and dawdled his note pad on his knee. Through one window he could see the vague outline of New York City's skyscrapers reaching up into the noonday smog of carbon monoxide and factory wastes. Through the window opposite him, across the spacious panelled room, he could see Newark, a distant blotch of buildings that seemed to blend together in a conglomerate of despair, but which he remembered with warmth.

And he was in Hudson, the land mass between them, separated by the Hudson and Hackensack Rivers, the opening of America. The room smelled faintly of aspen pine and an attractive, conservatively-dressed woman pored through a very fat and rather old book at her desk.

On the wall was a painting of strawberries that Remo did not know had been purchased the day before for five thousand dollars, but if told that, he would have believed it. The artist had the kind of vision beyond sight, the kind of control beyond genius.

Remo's plan was simple, as were most incipient disasters, he thought. He would make his presence known in town. He would annoy, browbeat and insult. Someone would come to him. And that someone would talk. It was a simple process. Unlike movie actors, people—brave people and cowardly people—would disclose anything to stop pain. The mysterious interrogation technique of the Russians consisted of punching people; Henry the 8th had them beaten with sticks; Genghis Khan ordered them kicked.

Only the mental defectives of Hollywood and Hitler found it necessary to use hot coals, organ crushers and skin peelers. Professionals just hit.

And if no one came after him, Remo would go after them. He'd start with the most likely candidate—Police Chief Brian Dugan, a man of ready wit and warmth, and a thief. According to CURE, he had paid $80,000 for his job from a previous administration. A man didn't pay that much for that job to bring law and order to a town. And if Dugan didn't have the lead, then it would be Verillio or Gasso or Palumbo or the mayor or the local editor, or any of the people whose names Smith had given him.

But that was Phase Two. This was Phase One, interviews and annoyance. And first on the list was Verillio who, according to CURE, was either the Mafia kingpin of Hudson and maybe the nation, or was just an unwitting dupe of Mafia interests.

Which was something like the report to the German general staff that the allies were going to land at Normandy on June 6, 1944. They had the exact time and the place. Fortunately, they also had thirty-nine other exact times and places ranging from Norway to the Balkans and from 1943 to 1946. So much for intelligence.

"I've got it," said the secretary. "I've got it."

Remo smiled. "Got what?"

"Shiva. I'm looking up Shiva." She began to read: "Shiva. One of the three major gods of Hinduism, also known as the destroyer." She looked up.

Remo was definitely interested. He had heard that word before. "I heard he was called the shatterer of worlds, too." He said slowly, from memory: "I am Shiva. . . ." but he could not remember the rest of it.

As he said that the door opened and a strong faced businessman poked his head out of the inner office.

"Joan, may I speak to you a moment, please? Oh, hello. You must be the magazine writer. I'll be with you in a minute."

"I've got Shiva for you right here," said the secretary.

"Destroyer of worlds, I am Shiva," said Remo.

"What?" said Verillio, his eyes widening.

"I was trying to remember a quote. I've got it now. 'I am created Shiva the Destroyer; death, the shatterer of worlds.' "

"Are you Shiva?" asked Verillio solemnly.

Remo laughed. "Me? No. I'm Remo Barry. I'm the magazine writer you spoke with last night."

"Oh, good. Be with you in a minute. Joan?"

Remo watched the secretary grab a pad and pencil and disappear into the office. In five minutes, he was allowed into the office and pretended to write down the canned corn Verillio was spewing. Hudson faced the problems of all other cities: fleeing industries, rising crime and welfare, and, of course, a lack of hope.

But Verillio saw great hope for Hudson. He saw great hope for nearly half an hour, then he invited Remo to lunch at the Casino at the Lake.

He saw hope through his baked stuffed clams and his veal Holstein. When Remo ordered rice, just rice, he became very interested. Why did Remo order just rice? Was it an eastern custom? A special fad diet? What was it?

"Would you believe I like rice, Mr. Verillio?"

"No," said Dominic Verillio.

"You acquire a taste for it."

"When you started eating it though, you didn't like it, right?"

"I didn't particularly like it."

"Then why did you start?"

"Why did you start eating baked stuffed clams?"

"Because I loved them."

Remo smiled and Verillio laughed.

Remo shrugged: "What can I say other than that you're a Mafioso?"

Verillio guffawed. "You know if it weren't so funny, it would be serious. I think that the Italian community at large suffers because of the greed of a few men of Italian ancestry. Doctors, lawyers, dentists, professors, salesmen, hard-working people like myself. I honestly believe that whenever the FBI has an unsolved crime, they arrest the first Italian they can lay their hands on. I honestly believe that. Are you Italian, of Italian ancestry, that is?"

"I might be. I don't know. I was raised in an orphanage."

"Where?"

"I'd rather not go into it. It's not too pleasant, not knowing who your mother and father are, not even knowing your ancestry."

"Could it be eastern? Oriental of some sort?"

"I don't think so. I figure the Mediterranean on the

south to Germany on the North, from Ireland on the west to Siberia on the east. That's kind of not knowing, isn't it?"

"You Catholic?" Verillio asked.

"You deal in heroin?"

Verillio did not laugh this time. "I think that's insulting. Now what did you mean?"

"I'm trying to find out if you're in the Mafia and if you deal in heroin."

"This is too insulting," said Verillio and threw his napkin down into the egg on top of his veal, gave Remo a hateful stare and left. So much for Verillio, Remo thought. One seed planted.

Police Chief Brian Dugan couldn't be needled. He dropped fifteen references to his standing in the Catholic church, the Little League, the "Clean Up—Paint Up—Fix Up" program, and community relations. He was very proud of his community relations program.

"We teach our police how to deal with them better."

Chief Brian Dugan sat behind his desk with a picture of Franklin Delano Roosevelt behind him. It was a desk cluttered with trophies, statue paperweights and an American flag on a little holder. The picture of Roosevelt had lost its color to the decades.

"Who's *them*?" Remo asked.

"Well, you know. *Them*. Urban problems."

"I don't know," said Remo and made squiggles on his pad with his pencil. He crossed a leg.

"You know. The colored. Blacks. Afro-Americans."

"*Them?*"

"Yeah. Them," said the chief proudly, his red face

beaming, his clear blue eyes twinkling, his freckled hands playing nervously with themselves.

"I hear your city is becoming the heroin capital of the nation." Remo watched the blue eyes. They didn't bat.

"Heroin is a problem," said the chief. "A growing national problem."

"What's your cut?"

"What?"

"What's your cut? Your rakeoff?" The tone was casual. The chief was not. He levelled a blue-eyed stare at Remo, his posture exuded integrity, his jaw showed courage. His lips tightened.

"Are you accusing me of being involved in the traffic of drugs?"

The tone was almost identical to that of Remo's former chief when Remo had been a patrolman in Newark and ticketed the patrol car sent around to collect the chief's Christmas liquor.

"Somebody's got to be protecting the drug traffic," Remo said.

"Are you accusing me?" demanded the chief.

"If the shoe fits, chief."

"Get out of here."

Remo didn't move.

"This interview is at an end," said the chief. "And I'd like to warn you there are laws against libel."

"Only if you print an untruth," Remo said and smiled. Then he got up and left. Another seed planted.

He walked out of the office, past the lieutenant who performed the duties of a clerk-typist, out into the hallway and waited for the elevator in the special mustiness that only a police station could manufacture. He wondered casually if his job would be necessary if police departments were better. But how could they be better? They didn't recruit from Mars. No, the police of any city reflected the morality of that city. No better, no worse. It took two to make a bribe.

The elevator door opened and Remo strolled in. It was a large elevator, the size of a small kitchen, apparently a good quarter-of-a-century old. He pressed *main floor*.

The bronzelike metal door closed, almost painfully slowly. With a cough, the elevator descended. It stopped at the next floor to let two detectives and a prisoner enter. One of the detectives, a drawn-faced man of Remo's height, wearing the standard fedora, saw Remo and said politely: "Hi."

Then the trio moved to the rear and Remo moved to the front. Remo had nodded, before he suddenly realized why he recognized the detective and the detective recognized him.

"Balls," thought Remo and attempted to keep his face forward toward the elevator door, hoping the detective would just be mildly troubled, trying to remember the face and then would forget it. Unfortunately, the policeman's trade, especially the detective's, did not allow for the casual filing of faces in the memory. At least not the competent ones. Remo hoped that Bill Skorich had not developed competence.

Remo remembered their first year together on the force in Newark and how Skorich would forget little things and always end up on the short end of conversations with the desk sergeant, the detectives, the lieutenant and the captain. He never fouled up enough to stand before the chief.

Yet, although negative feedback was not the best training device in the world, it most certainly was a training device. Either the person adjusted to the abuse or he adjusted himself so that there was no more abuse. If Skorich had adjusted himself, he was about to be a dead man.

Out of the corner of his eye, Remo saw Skorich take a step to the front. He was examining the side of Remo's face. He took another step dragging the prisoner a step forward with him, and the detective on the other end moved a half step.

Remo couldn't hide his face and then run for it, not in police headquarters. It would be a great way to get your picture circulated, especially after the conversation with the chief.

So Remo turned slowly to Bill Skorich and hoped that the plastic surgery on his cheekbones and nose would do the trick, and he looked Skorich in the eye and then appeared confused. As he did this, he silently prayed: "Bill, be a foul-up. C'mon, baby. Don't do it right. Not now."

Skorich's drawn face twisted in confusion and Remo's heart suddenly became light. "Attaway to go, Billy baby," he thought. "That's it. Beautiful. Nobody remembers a dead man's face. Especially after plastic surgery."

Then Skorich's face lighted up, a smile with it, that quickly turned into shock at seeing a dead man alive. And Remo knew that Skorich knew.

The last word Detective William Skorich of the Newark Police Department said was not a word. It was the beginning of a name.

The sound was "Re. . . ."

Using Skorich's body as a shield, out of view of the prisoner and the other bull, Remo shot a finger into Skorich's solar plexus, driving the finger in deep, up into the heart, rupturing muscles and valves. All in just the time it took to say "Re. . . ."

It was the floater stroke where the hand floated free of the momentum of the body and moved itself. It had the advantage of stopping talk immediately.

Skorich's eyes widened and before he slumped, Remo's hands were in his own pockets with the note pad tucked under an arm. Skorich collapsed into Remo and Remo let himself be knocked to the far side of the elevator, saying, "Watch yourself, buddy."

Skorich brought the prisoner down on him as he fell. The fedora plopped over and the other detective, spinning like the far end of a whipping chain, stumbled onto it and then down onto the prisoner on top of the dead man on the floor of the elevator.

The doors opened on the main floor. Remo regained his balance, brushing himself off and stormed out of the elevator, yelling loudly, "I've been assaulted by a police officer. I've been assaulted right here in headquarters. Is that how you treat the press?"

Remo stood at the entrance of the elevator, pointing to the pile of bodies. The living detective was trying to raise himself and the prisoner both.

"There," yelled Remo. "That's him on the bottom. I want to press charges, right now. He pushed me."

It took the desk lieutenant three minutes to ascertain the situation, ten seconds to yell for an ambulance and three minutes with the faggy, pinko magazine writer to convince the writer that he had not been assaulted, but that the detective had fallen into

70

him because he was dead, probably with a heart attack.

"Dead?" said Remo, his mouth open, his eyes wide with terror.

"Yeah. Dead. You know. What happens to us pigs when we try to protect you. Another pig dead, buddy."

"I . . . I don't know what to say," Remo said.

"Just try looking before you jump to conclusions. That's all. Just try looking. Just a little, fair look."

"I . . . I'm sorry," said Remo and there was no act to his sadness. It was very real and when he left the station, he felt very much like a drink, but you do not take a drink when you are on peak, you do not take it even when you come off peak. You treat yourself like an alcoholic because that's the business.

And when you pass a bar and see yourself in the reflection of the window, you're glad you can deny yourself something you want very much. And you hate the face looking back at you and moving along with you.

Because, Remo Williams, you're lower than an animal. You're a machine. An animal kills to eat and live. A man kills because he's frightened or sick or he's told to and he's afraid not to. But you, Remo Williams, you kill because that's what the machine was designed to do.

Remo crossed the street, where the red-headed cop directed traffic with a sure hand born of experience, and walked past a donut store where youngsters jammed around the counter in their after-school gluttony ritual. He would have liked, at that moment, to have Smith in his hands and to break Smith's arms and to say to Smith, "That's what pain feels like,

71

Smitty. That's where it's at, little adding machine."
Now he knew why he sometimes hated Smith. Because they were alike. Twin peas in a sick pod. And they did their jobs right.

The youngsters inside the doughnut store jostled playfully. A young black girl and a young white girl, their books clasped firmly to their budding breasts, giggled and looked at a young black man in floppy hat, white twill shirt and flared pants who held something out to them in his fist. He was laughing too, taunting them.

He wiggled his clenched fist and threw back his head laughing. The two girls exchanged glances, then giggled again. The glance said: "Should we?"

The white girl reached out to the black hand holding something. The hand withdrew. She shrugged. The hand went forward again, and opened up. It held a small glassine envelope. The black boy laughed. The white girl snatched the envelope and laughed.

And Remo thought of the picture of the OD that Smith had shown him on the cruise ship. And suddenly, he didn't feel so bad about being a machine.

The mayor and the editor were next.

CHAPTER SEVEN

Willie the Plumber Palumbo had been told not to worry. He had been told not to worry by Don Dominic Verillio. He had been told that twice that afternoon.

So Willie the Plumber went to the Oyster Cove Bar and drank three old-fashioneds to buck up his courage.

When Willie the Plumber was told not to worry by anyone, he worried. When he was told not to worry by Don Dominic Verillio, he often had trouble containing his bladder.

So he spent much of the afternoon helping himself not to worry with the old-fashioneds. And by 3 p.m., he was not worrying all that much. He knew that he would not have a care by midnight if he kept at it, but he also knew that by dawn he would be burdened with an overabundance of troubles if he did not put down the last old-fashioned and do what he had to do.

Since Willie the Plumber was a man of understanding and compromise, a man who knew that others had to live also—his philosophy behind bribes—he was not too overly harsh on himself. He ordered one more old-fashioned and drank half of it, leaving a dollar tip for the bartender.

He went outside where his blue Cadillac Eldorado occupied the previously empty space in front of the fire hydrant and removed the parking ticket from the windshield. He could get it discounted to $5 from $25, and a parking lot four blocks away would have cost him $4. Besides, getting a ticket fixed reaffirmed his status to his compatriots and himself.

Willie the Plumber opened the unlocked door of his car, dropped the ticket in the glove compartment on top of a small pile of tickets. He got them cleared once a month when he paid all his monthly bills. Willie the Plumber did not have to lock his car. Only nobodies locked their cars.

The blue Eldorado gleamed with a just polished shine. He had the car polished every day by a car wash near his house, the engine checked every month by the Cadillac dealer, and had it tuned up every six weeks. His cars never failed him.

He was a thin man with a racking cough that, no matter how violent, failed to even jar the ash on the end of the eternal cigarette he held in his mouth. He saw the dentist when the pain was so bad he couldn't sleep and the doctor twice—once when he thought he was going blind and another time when he thought he was dying. From time to time he would pass out.

For this condition he would consult a druggist who would tell him to consult a doctor. Willie always said he would, and got in return some powder or pills, or some drops.

"Passing out," he once explained, "is just nature's way of telling you to slow down."

He put the key in the ignition, blanked out momentarily, then started the car. It purred. It moved with graceful ease into the traffic.

He drove through the commercial district and then turned, going past tree-shaded private homes, two stories and two families. He hit the main boulevard and turned left, down toward the southern end of the county. Five blocks past the brick and aluminum buildings of St. Luke's College, a Jesuit school done in twentieth century garden-apartment architecture, he turned right down a block of elegant homes with old oak and maple trees in front, wide, strong and rich. The homes were tudor and colonial, with a natural manicure to the lawns, and a cleanliness and brightness that came only with expensive maintenance.

Willie the Plumber pulled to the curb and stopped the car. He lit another cigarette from the one in his mouth, then carefully put the dwindling butt out in the car ashtray next to the radio-stereo-tape system.

He swung his $85 Florsheims out onto the street, and got up by throwing himself after them. He breathed deeply. He did not pass out. That little triumph behind him, he shut the door of his blue El-dorado.

He walked purposefully around the front grille inspecting it as he passed. There was a smudge near the left headlight. Willie took his blue handkerchief out of his coat pocket and bent down, wiping at the smudge. It came off, thank goodness. He coughed up some brownish-red substance which lodged deep in the grille. Willie kneeled down and pushed the handkerchief into the grille to get at whatever it was he had coughed out. The grille cleaned, he rose, and feeling dizzy for a moment, waited.

75

Then he walked again, past a lawn sign that said "Rosenberg" to the steps of a tudor-style house with wood beams lacing off dappled white cement.

He rang the doorbell. A stocky woman in a knit suit answered the bell.

"Oh, it's you," she said. "Just a minute. I'll see if he's home."

Willie the Plumber heard Mrs. Edith Rosenberg walk up a flight of steps to the second floor. She had left the door open.

He heard her knock. "Gaetano?" came her voice.

"Yes, Mrs. Rosenberg," said a deep muffled voice.

"That awful man is here to see you again. The skinny one who coughs."

"Oh. Okay, send him up. Thank you, Mrs. Rosenberg."

"You really shouldn't associate with such people, a nice boy like yourself."

The nice boy Mrs. Rosenberg referred to was the quiet man who rented the second floor, who shared Friday night dinners with the Rosenbergs, who would listen to how her family wasn't worthy of her and how Mr. Rosenberg thought of nothing but the business.

The nice boy, Willie the Plumber knew, was Gaetano Gasso, Verillio's enforcer, whom everyone called Mr. Gasso, who did not have a name like Ducks or Bananas or the Plumber, because no one would venture testing one out, even when Mr. Gasso were not present.

Mr. Gasso could freeze people by looking at them. Mr. Gasso did not like putting guns in people's faces and then pulling the trigger, although he would do that if there were no other avenue available to him.

Mr. Gasso liked to pull off arms and legs. Mr. Gasso liked to blend other people's skulls with chairs and tables, with sides of walls when appropriate.

Mr. Gasso liked to crack ribs. Mr. Gasso liked people to fight back. He liked them to fight back with fists or clubs or guns. For guns, he used guns. But sometimes he used cars. Cars were good against guns. When cars drove into people standing against walls who used guns, they made cracking sounds from the chest down. Then Mr. Gasso would finish what was left, and pull the glass splinters from his own face.

One time he pulled a bullet out of his face. But Mr. Gasso didn't stop using cars. One time, while ameliorating a Teamster dispute, Mr. Gasso was hit in the face by a truck driver with a sledge hammer. The truck driver was put back together with wires and through great perseverance became one of the really great wheelchair basketball players, although his left hand dribble was never much good, because he had no nerves left in that hand. Mr. Gasso knew his jaw was broken a week later, when he bit into a Tootsie Roll.

People did not tend to joke with Mr. Gasso or make disparaging remarks. Even people who did not know who he was. There was always a table open for Mr. Gasso at nightclubs and restaurants, although he never tipped.

Willie the Plumber did not allow himself to believe, not even to suspect, that he did not like Mr. Gasso very much. He loved Mr. Gasso. But every time he had to deliver a message to Mr. Gasso, he would fortify himself first with old-fashioneds. One time it took three-and-a-half days for Willie to take a message to Mr. Gasso because Don Dominic had said

77

do this thing when you have time. Today, however, he had told Willie it was urgent and that Willie should not worry.

Mrs. Rosenberg clomped downstairs.

"He'll see you," she said with disgust, and let Willie enter.

Willie was polite to Mrs. Rosenberg. He thanked her profusely. He was not exactly sure how Mr. Gasso felt about his landlady. Willie the Plumber was not about to experiment.

He walked up the gray carpeted flight of steps to the second floor and knocked on the white painted door.

"Come in," said Mr. Gasso.

Willie entered, closing the door behind him. It was a well-lit room with wide bay windows, soft plush furniture, a 27-inch color television set, and doilies over everything. Even a bedspread made of white doilies. Mr. Gasso made the doilies with little hooked needles and some sort of thread or string. Needless to say, his strange hobby failed to draw ridicule.

Mr. Gasso occasionally gave doilies to people he knew. When you got a doily from Mr. Gasso you put it on the most noticeable thing closest to your door lest Mr. Gasso should happen to visit you and happen to ask you what you did with his doily. Or worse, not ask.

Mr. Gasso sat on the edge of his doily covered bed, in his underwear. He had shoulders like cement drums used to anchor bridge supports. These shoulders extended to arms like steel beams. The arms ended at table sized fists. There were no wrists, just the giant arms ending in giant hands. All of this was covered with thick black hair from the top of his

78

bulky head down to his ankles. His ankles and his palms and the soles of his feet were the only parts of Mr. Gasso's body not covered with hair—if you didn't count eyeballs and tongue. Mr. Gasso had hair on his lips.

His ankles looked as if someone had massaged them with a depilatory. Or maybe he could pull off his hair like long underwear, and it was a bad fit at the ankles.

Mr. Gasso apparently felt no embarrassment about his body hair. At least his peer group had never ostracized him for it.

"It's so good to see you, Mr. Gasso," said Willie the Plumber.

Mr. Gasso concentrated on his stitching. "What do you want?" he said.

"Don Dominic needs your help."

"Why didn't he come himself?"

"That's the problem, Mr. Gasso. He thinks someone is on to the big thing."

"He doesn't want to see me."

"Oh no, Mr. Gasso. He'd love to see you. Really. He has great respect for you, like we all do, Mr. Gasso. But there's this magazine writer who he wants to play it smart with. Like we keep a tail on him, and we get you to size him up and then if we need you, you know."

"I know," said Mr. Gasso.

Willie the Plumber smiled a very sincere and honest smile of true joy.

"Did he say anything about this guy?"

And it was here that Willie fought for control of his bladder. From time to time, certain people were sent to Mr. Gasso with messages. Sometimes the mes-

79

sage meant for Mr. Gasso to kill the hit, but sometimes it meant for Mr. Gasso to hit the messenger.
Willie the Plumber had to be very careful with the
words lest he say a wrong one and suffer for it. Then
again, he might get everything right and still suffer
for it.

Willie said very slowly:

"He said this guy was a butterfly so be careful of
the wings. That's what he said."

Mr. Gasso cast his dull brown eyes on Willie. Willie was smiling very broadly.

"He said that?"

"Yes sir," said Willie as if the tidings could have
nothing to do with his personal safety.

"Okay. This is what you do. You set up the sizing
and you get Johnny the Duck, and Vinnie O'Boyle.
They'll be the tail. And get Pops Smith, the colored
guy. I like him real good."

"You really want a nigger on this?" asked Willie
the Plumber.

"A lot of niggers is better than you. A lot of niggers is good people. I trust Pops Smith. I don't trust
you, Willie the Plumber. We'll meet at the Monarch
Bar in half an hour."

"I like Pops Smith. I like him. I like him real good.
I'll get Pops Smith."

"Shut the door on your way out, Willie the Plumber."

"Awfully nice seeing you again, Mr. Gasso."

"Yeah," said Mr. Gasso and Willie was out the
door in an instant. He shut it quietly, but quickly,
and bounced down the steps, thanking Mrs. Rosenberg and saying how nice it was to meet her again;
what a lovely home she had and weren't those splen-

80

did doilies she had on her sofa, why Willie had one just like it at home.

"I use them because it makes Gaetano feel needed," said Mrs. Rosenberg sharply. "Good day."

"Good day, Mrs. Rosenberg," said Willie the Plumber. Then it was into his beautiful Eldorado and thence to the Monarch bar and an old-fashioned which he brought into the telephone booth.

"Hello, O'Boyle. Willie the Plumber. I want you at the Monarch now. Don't give me that shit about you being in the saddle. If you don't pull out now, you may never be able to use it again."

Willie the Plumber hung up, waited for the disconnect, deposited a dime, then dialed again.

"Pops Smith . . . oh, it's you. This is Willie the Plumber. Get your black ass over to the Monarch now. I can go what? Are you coming over now? You want me to tell that to Gaetano? You want I should let him know you told him to go fuck himself? Yeah, he wants you. And make it snappy."

Willie hung up and when he heard the disconnect, spoke loudly into the mouthpiece, "nigger."

Then he dialed again. "Johnny? How are you? This is Willie the Plumber. Got something good for you. I'm at the Monarch. Yeah, Mr. Gasso would like you to come. Okay, but hurry if you can."

Then Willie hung up and strode to the bar, looked around menacingly at the workingmen and city hall officials, ignoring the eyes of the two plainclothesmen at the far end of the bar.

He was going to have real respect soon. Didn't he arrange for the drivers of the Ocean Wheels trucks? Didn't he direct them to the warehouse where Mr. Gasso took over? Hadn't he kept his mouth shut when they never came back, even though one of them was his brother, and his sister-in-law had thrown a pot of hot pasta at his head when the brother never reappeared?

So he didn't know where the big shipment was. You couldn't tell everyone. But he knew a lot of things. Like he knew Verillio had a boss and that it wasn't Verillio who planned the big drug import.

Willie the Plumber knew, because on certain key moves, Verillio would close the door, make a telephone call, and then come out with his decision.

Willie the Plumber knew, but he was telling no one, until the time was just right. Then, he'd have some respect.

He pulled a roll of bills out of his pocket to let the bartender and customers ogle, then peeled off two tens.

"Get the bar a drink," said Willie the Plumber, who one day soon would do to the perfect human weapon what Gaetano Gasso and squads of men could never do.

CHAPTER EIGHT

Remo left the taxicab at city hall and noticed the two cars of hoods sizing him up. Dugan or Verillio. He would bet on Verillio. Dugan could have used his cops. Whoops. On the far side of the street, plainclothesmen in an unmarked squad car. Well, Dugan *and* Verillio.

"All's well that begins well," he thought. Up the well-worn city hall steps he bounced, stopped to give one and all a profile, then went into the building. A candy and soft drink stand was to his right. Clerk's office to his far right. Tax office on his left. Mayor's office, according to the black and gold sign in the middle of the double staircase, up one flight.

Up one flight he went, glancing into the city council chambers where democracy and various other kinds of public stealing occurred. The difference between a democracy and a dictatorship, he thought, is that thieves tend to rotate more in a democracy. But the thieves in a democracy had to be organized.

If he believed this way, what the hell was he doing in his job? he asked himself.

He already knew the answer. The same thing ninety per cent of the rest of the world was doing in its jobs. He did his job because that was what he did and no exploration of his inner psyche ever provided a better explanation.

He read the sign, *Mayor's Office,* knocked, and walked in. A very attractive, gray-haired woman sat at a typewriter in the outer office.

"Can I help you?" she said.

"Yes. My name's Remo Barry. I'm the magazine writer. I've come for my appointment with Mayor Hansen."

"Oh, yes, we've been expecting you," said the secretary who, Remo thought, should give lessons on aging. She was a stunning woman with white hair, fine features and an alive face that was young despite lines.

She pressed a button and a door opened. It was not the mayor who appeared, unless the mayor had suddenly become five-feet-eight and was built like the Venus deMilo with a face of fine-cut living marble. The young woman had blondish hair with streaks, deep-brown eyes and a smile that would collapse a monk.

She wore a black leather skirt and a form-fitting gray sweater without bra, beads dangling over breasts. And for the first time since he had taken sex instructions, those dragging daily muscle and mental controls that Chiun had foisted on him, Remo felt an urge rising within him.

He dropped the pad over his fly.

"You're Remo Barry," said the woman. "I'm Cynthia Hansen, the mayor's daughter and secretary. I'm glad you came."

"Yeah," said Remo, surprised to find himself thinking that he could take the woman now, in the ante room to the mayor's office, then flee and probably never get caught.

This was not a healthy thing to think, although it was the most pleasant idea he had entertained in months. But it would be a very nice way to be very dead. He refocused his thoughts and breathed deeply of the oxygen in the air, resting his consciousness on the eternal forces of the universe. It didn't do much, however, for his erection and he entered her office with his pad still genitally oriented. Then he got mad at himself, forced blood control, and it was gone.

Good. He felt strong and in charge. He obviously had had a similar effect upon the woman, because it became evident through the gray sweater that she was aroused too.

He would play that. He would use her arousal against her, pushing the line of conversation into areas she did not want to go, but would have to go because he was in command.

The office was relatively bare but for a desk, three chairs, a couch and political photographs on the wall. The blind was drawn.

She sat down on the couch and crossed her legs.

"Well," she said, fondling her beads, "where shall we begin?"

So much for blood control and the salvation of America and its constitution.

"Here," cried Remo and he was on her, his hands into the sweater, his body between her legs, forcing his mouth on hers, abandoning everything he had been taught. Just taking. And before he knew it, he was in her, she had put him in. And then, bang, it was over for both of them. Seven-second sex. A textbook disaster.

He smelled her perfume and felt close to the smooth skin of her cheek. She had not even removed her clothes. Neither had Remo.

He kissed her cheek.

"Don't do that," she said. "It was good. But don't do that."

"Yeah," said Remo and removed himself and zipped up, as Cynthia Hansen smoothed out her skirt.

"Well, now," she said as if nothing had happened, "where shall we begin?"

"At the beginning," said Remo. "Tell me about Hudson."

He settled down in a chair and began to take notes. Cynthia Hansen began her peroration as though the last minute had not existed.

She told how corruption had been endemic to Hudson, how the city had begun to die in the 1930s under one boss and how he was replaced by another boss who was worse because he was inept. She told of two decades of corruption, shuffling of governments, but nothing changing.

Then, just eighteen months ago, the city government had been decimated by indictments and convictions. There was an election, probably the last time Hudson would have a chance to redeem itself.

Her father, Craig Hansen, had faced another organization hack and an out-and-out Mafia thug, but please don't quote her on that.

Well, her father had won, barely won and now with the new election for a four year term, the city might have turned the corner.

"You see, Mr. Barry, he may not have wrought miracles in eighteen months, but he has brought hope. He is a dreamer, Mr. Barry, in a city shorn of

86

dreams. He is a doer in a city governed, til now by the fix. In short, Mr. Barry, Craig Hansen is the last hope of this city. I think that tells it about as it is."

"How does he feel about being mayor of the heroin capital of the country?"

"What do you mean?"

"You know, the rakeoff from the big heroin imports. How does he stand on that?"

Cynthia Hansen laughed.

"Mr. Barry, you're a very attractive man. But please, that's just absurd. Yes, we, like other cities, have a heroin problem. But we're finding new and more relevant ways to deal with that problem. Storefront therapy centers. My father is finding more relevant ways to deal with minority communities. Granted, with the means at his disposal and the apparent reluctance of the government to produce massive aid, progress is limited, but we feel it is meaningful and relevant."

"What about your father's personal involvement with the heroin trade?"

Cynthia Hansen shook her head and looked quizzically at Remo. "I beg your pardon?"

"You know, the big heroin deal. Stuff may be worth a billion dollars for all we know. Your father's involvement in it?"

"Just who the hell are you?"

"You ought to know. You checked me out."

"What are you after?"

"Story on heroin."

"Your editor told me it was to be a story on Hudson."

"It is. Heroin capital of the United States."

"Well, I'm sorry. There's nothing I can tell you

about heroin that you couldn't read in any newspaper. Now would you care to discuss some of our basic urban problems?"

"Yeah. How are you going to get the heroin out?"

"Good day, Mr. Barry," said Cynthia Hansen dropping her fist to the couch on which they had made love and pushing herself up from it.

As she stepped toward the door, quick strong paces, vibrant strutting hips, firm young breasts, a face so classic it looked as if it fell off a Roman wall, Remo reached out for a wrist and flipped her back on the couch. This time he was going to do it better.

This time he took off his clothes and hers. He arranged her carefully on the couch. He was tender and gentle and he remembered all Chiun's tricks. He did not neglect the backs of her knees or the insides of her ears or the hair at the base of the neck.

He brought her along with him, slowly but fully, and when she was at a peak, he brought her to a higher peak, and then another higher peak until she could control herself no longer and exploded in a violent paroxysm of passion, shuddering convulsively down the length of her body.

And Remo put his face close to her ear and whispered gently, "What about the heroin?"

"HEROIN," she groaned in exultant relief. Remo felt her body tremble again. He had misjudged the timing again. Still time to salvage something. Maybe tenderness. So he nibbled her right ear, and whispered into it, "You know, hon. Who's dealing?"

"I just wanted you for your body, handsome," said Cynthia Hansen with a triumphant chuckle. "Women's lib frees a lot of us."

"Cynthia, did you ever realize how stupid you look when you come?"

"No. I'm enjoying it too much to entertain those self-defeating thoughts."

Remo kissed her once more, this time for real, then left her and got dressed in the office as he watched her dress. She took forty seconds to put on her braless sweater, panties and black leather skirt. Then she put on makeup for seven minutes.

"Why don't you come around tomorrow about the same time, Remo. I like your body."

"I don't do this all the time for nothing."

"There's money in the upper right hand drawer."

Remo laughed. "Somehow I get the feeling I might get pregnant from this."

He opened her office door and stepped out.

"See you tomorrow," she called after him.

"How about the interview with the mayor?"

"His schedule is filled. Sorry."

"I'll see him. Don't worry."

"Will you come back tomorrow?"

"No," Remo said.

"Okay," she said. "You come back tomorrow and you can see him for five minutes. Get here at 10 a.m. and you can see him at noon. We'll find some way to while away the hours. Now shut the door. I've got work to do."

Another seed planted. Remo smiled to himself as he thought of the double meaning. On to the editor.

Editor James Horgan sat with his feet on his desk, his polka dot bowtie open over his checked shirt, cleaning his fingernails with a makeup rule, a thin strip of steel used to separate type in the composing room.

"Sure I know about the massive heroin import. I imported it. I want to start my kids early on the habit and since the stuff is so hard to get nowadays, I thought I'd buy a lifetime supply. Anything else you want to know?"

"I'm serious, Mr. Horgan."

"You don't sound it." The voice was a gravelly whine, a pervasive discontent in search of something to be discontented about. Horgan got the pinky with a right-angle tip of the makeup rule.

"Hudson has become the heroin capital of the country. I believe you're the mastermind," Remo said.

Horgan looked up. His eyes twinkled.

"You're on a fishing expedition, son. What do you really want?"

"I want the facts."

"All right. There's a market for heroin. As long as there's a market, you're going to have people selling it. As long as it is illegal it will be expensive and the people who sell it will be criminals. Now if you could buy the stuff with a prescription from your doctor, goodbye heroin traffic."

"But wouldn't that create addicts?"

"You talk as if we don't have them now. What that would do would be to make it unprofitable for the pushers and they'd stop trying to get other people hooked," Horgan said.

"Wouldn't that turn America into a nation of drug-users?"

"As opposed to?"

"Is that why you imported so much heroin?"

"I've gone fishing myself, son. You're not bad at it.

90

Then again, you're not very good at it. Ever been in the newspaper business?"

"No," said Remo. "There are some things I wouldn't stoop to, even for money."

Horgan guffawed. "What makes you think we get paid?"

Remo rose to leave. "Thank you for the interview," he said. "I'll keep you in mind."

"Uh, look, son. Good luck on whatever you're looking for and on the way out, try to wake up my city desk. See if any of my editors are alive and send one of them in. You can tell they're alive if the dust hasn't settled on their faces. And if you should bump into anyone who can write, tell him he's hired. You wouldn't want a job, would you?"

"No thanks. I've got one."

Remo walked out into the dull, green city room, lathered by ink dust. Around a collection of desks pushed together sat a group of men, moving their hands zombie-like over pieces of paper.

Physically, they were alive.

Outside, in front of the Hudson Tribune in Hudson Square, Remo picked up his tails. He took a taxi to New York City instead of a bus or the subway, so that his tails would have an easier time staying with him.

He brought them to a modern apartment building in the fashionable upper East Side of New York City.

He knew that his tails would be all over the doorman with five, ten, maybe twenty dollar bills. Of course, in such an exclusive neighborhood, no doorman would give away information for five dollars. They might even want as much as fifty. Remo hoped the doorman held out for top dollar.

On the tenth floor, he got out of the elevator and walked down the carpeted foyer to his apartment.

When he entered, he saw Chiun sitting before the television set, the flickering making his yellow face pale in the darkness of the apartment.

CURE had bought Chiun a taping device, which he brought with him when he accompanied Remo. This way, he could tape the daytime soap operas instead of missing two while he watched one.

"It is wrong," he had complained, "that all the good shows should come at one time so that they be missed. Why do they not have one after another so people can have true enjoyment?"

With his taping device hooked up to another television in the apartment, Chiun could watch his soap operas from noon until 7 p.m. He would make little clucking sounds as Mrs. Claire Wentworth disclosed that her daughter had been living with Dr. Bruce Barton, even though Dr. Barton could not leave his wife, Jennifer, because she was dying of leukemia, and even though Loretta, the daughter, was really in love with Vance Masterman who, she did not realize, was her father but who she thought was in league with Professor Singbar Ramkwat of the Pakistani Embassy who had stolen the plans for the lymph-node cure which Bart Henderson had devoted his life to developing before he met Loretta, with whom he was in love.

As Remo remembered it, this was pretty much where Mrs. Wentworth and Vance Masterman were a year and a half ago. He mentioned it to Chiun, as he went to the phone on the living room table.

"Quiet," said Chiun.

Remo dialed a number, let it ring three times, then

put the receiver down on the cradle and reached into a drawer for a plastic box punctured for speaker holes. The white plastic box had four dials on the left side, each with numbers one through nine.

What was that combination again? He knew it as well as his birthday, mainly because it was his birthday, minus two digits from the year. He dialed the number, setting the box on function. When the phone rang, he lifted the receiver and snapped the box onto it, transforming the meaningless squawks into a human voice.

Unfortunately, the voice was always Harold W. Smith's, and Remo liked the squawks better. Outside telephone booths had become almost open circuits because of the little known but extensive tapping of them by security agencies. And those that weren't tapped didn't work, a fact which drove the Mafia to write threatening letters to the telephone supervisors. So now, Remo used a scrambler.

"Yeah," Remo said.

"Still no shipments have moved out, and the buyers around the country are getting edgy. We've heard this around. How are you doing?"

"Okay for the first day. I've created some interest."

"Good."

"Are you running those heroin detectors through Hudson?" Remo asked.

"Yeah, but we've gotten nothing. The stuff may be underground and if so we wouldn't pick it up. What's wrong? You sound down."

"I saw an old friend today."

"Oh, that thing. Yes, we got a report on it. Well, we expected you might run into something like that."

"I'm glad we did, you sonofabitch," said Remo

and hung up the phone. Then he dialed the number again, but took off the scrambler and listened to the receiver squawk incoherently.

At 7:35, Chiun turned off the last of his daytime serials and put Remo through his workout. He noted that Remo had had sex twice by certain alterations in his movements, and he advised against orgasms while at peak.

They went through the floater stroke again, with warnings again from Chiun about target balance and the dangers of missing the target.

At 10:15 p.m., Chiun made himself dinner and Remo showered, put his hand through a wall in frustration and went to bed. Skorich had been a nice guy.

CHAPTER NINE

Rad Pulmetter had his master's degree in agricultural biology, specifically the transmutation of wheat strains. With that sort of education, you either got on top of a tractor, joined Ralston Purina or went to work for one of the government agencies. Unless, of course, you wanted to teach agriculture which Rad Pulmetter did not want to do.

Which he used to explain to himself while asking himself what he was doing in the Hackensack meadows on a small platform similar to a duck blind, pointing an aluminum housed tube at passing vehicles and making notes. He made notes on blinks. He made notes largely on vegetable trucks. Why the Department of Agriculture needed a routing plan on tubers was beyond him. The stupidity of the government.

This day, he noted that government mail trucks were carrying tubers. Which was odd, because there must be better ways to ship carrots than by first class mail. He tried to explain that to his superior, but he was a new man who showed large areas of ignorance when it came to agriculture. But then politics was politics and sometimes it was whom you knew, not what you knew.

How many blinks per truck? his superior asked.
"About fifty. I don't know. I didn't think pumpkin pies or what have you were that important."

Thank you, Mr. Pulmetter, that will be all.

Soon after, a postal supervisor was also reassured of governmental stupidity when he was ordered to let the Department of Agriculture check all outgoing mail through a special machine.

The reports all finally reached a lemon-faced man with eyeglasses, sitting behind a desk in Folcroft Sanatorium in Rye, New York, the Long Island Sound magnificent in the dawn sunlight behind him.

The reports showed a clear pattern to Dr. Harold W. Smith's studied eyes. The heroin was still hidden. But the outlets were sealed off. The buyers had been screaming for it, and now attempts were being made to smuggle out small amounts through the mail, by personal carriers—what have you.

But the buyers were angry and they confirmed a suspicion. It was all Mafia and the *capo Mafioso* was Dominic Verillio. A solid confirmation. No doubt about it.

Harold Smith picked up his special phone and dialed. The phone rang and then was answered. There was squawking. Remo was either having trouble or playing games with the scrambler again. Almost by the month, the man showed signs of psychological deterioration.

Remo did not know it but CURE had twice tried to get men as standbys. Same method. But the drug that simulated death had produced death. Twice. The laboratories examined it and came back with the report that indeed it was a deadly poison.

"Could a man take it and live?"

96

"Doubtful. And if he did live, you'd have a vegetable," was the answer.

Smith never revealed this to Remo and especially not to Remo's trainer, Chiun. The old man already babbled on too much about Oriental gods taking the bodies of dead people and seeking revenge on evildoers.

Remo was a typical, overemotional, spiritually self-indulgent, American wise guy. Nothing Oriental about him. The only communing he did was with his stomach, sex organ and ego. He had all the calm Eastern spirituality of a hamburger and coke, to go.

A click on the phone and then a voice.

"Yeah. Whaddya want?"

"It's Verillio. He's definitely the Mafia man."

"It's 7:30 a.m."

"Well, I didn't want to miss you."

"Well, you didn't."

Click.

CHAPTER TEN

Don Dominic Verillio arrived at his office early that morning. He did not say hello to his secretary. He walked into his office, shut the door and without taking off his straw hat, sat down behind his desk and began drawing diagrams and plans, with arrows and boxes, much as he had learned in Officer's Candidate School during the Second World War. He had refined his strategy much since being mustered out in 1945 as a major with three battle citations.

He was going to play it smart. He would hold back Gaetano Gasso for the writer, Remo Barry. Barry knew something, was responsible for something, or belonged to something or someone. Gaetano Gasso would find out exactly what.

The winner, however, is usually he who commits his reserves last. That would mean sending in lightweight people first against Remo Barry's old Oriental servant. They would seize him, have him phone Barry. The gook's life for information from Remo Barry.

And if that did not pry out the information, then Gasso would take it out of Remo Barry's flesh. In pieces. So much for that.

To the other *capos*, he would say, wait. Yes, there had been trouble with delivery. There would be a new, better method of delivery shortly. Hold on. Your money is safe. So much for the *capos*.

He picked up the phone and dialed, apologized for the break in procedure and asked for an appointment because of an urgent matter. His voice was tender and respectful.

"I'll tell you everything when I get there. Yes. Well, I don't know. Okay, I'll meet you there."

On his way to his car, Don Dominic Verillio met Willie the Plumber Palumbo at a prearranged corner. Willie stood there coughing, next to his car.

Don Dominic explained what he wanted done, what Gaetano Gasso should do, what the other men would do.

"I'd like to go after the little gook myself," said Willie the Plumber when he heard that Mr. Gasso would not be going.

"No, I need you here."

Willie the Plumber bowed to Don Dominic Verillio and walked dizzily around the front of his car, to begin to deliver the messages. His footing was never good at this time of the day because of what he called "the mornings."

For a while he had asked people if they suffered from "the mornings" also—this to prove that losing consciousness when walking during the morning was a normal occurrence. When he received negative responses and advice that he should see a doctor, Willie the Plumber Palumbo stopped asking people if they, too, had the "mornings."

Verillio watched Willie the Plumber drive away, then continued walking to his own car. He drove off to the western side of the city, then through a large set of stone gates and parked his four-door gray Lincoln Continental Mark II before a crypt with a winged statue in marble.

He waited, then saw the familiar black car pull up behind his. He got out, walked around and sat in the passenger's seat.

His conference took only minutes. Then he strolled back to his car, opened the door and eased himself into the soft leather cushioning. He picked up the telephone, as he watched the black car move away in his rear-view mirror. He dialed his office number.

"Hello, Joan. I will be seeing this morning the editor of the *Tribune*, Chief Dugan and Mayor Hansen. If anyone phones, I will return their calls this afternoon."

He hung up and drove through the city to the back of the *Tribune* building, where trucks were loading the first edition. It was his city. His numbers, his whores and his narcotics. And he wasn't going to give it up because a few little things went wrong.

The brain would straighten out everything and then it would be his country, just as this was his city. He could count on that brilliant mind to do it. Even if that mind were not qualified for membership in the Sicilian Brotherhood.

But then he was not *Capo Mafioso* because he listened to the old pistol Petes and their hand kissing and vendettas, codes of this and codes of that, and all the hogwash imported from Sicily.

America still had the best killing systems and America had the best organizing systems. One should use them. And that way one could become the youngest *Capo Mafioso* ever. Only fifty-one and he was number one.

Well, that one person was above him but that person didn't count, not having the qualifications for the Sicilian Brotherhood.

Meanwhile, on the other side of town, Willie the Plumber spotted a meek looking man with a funny tubular device standing inside a truck and pointing the device at people.

Willie decided he didn't like the meek little man pointing that thing at his blue Eldorado. Maybe it would do something to the paint or something.

Willie the Plumber pulled up in front of the truck and parked so that the truck could not move. Then, rocking through another attack of "the mornings," he got out of the car and walked back to the man in the truck.

"Hey, whaddya doing in the truck with that thing?" asked Willie the Plumber.

"Department of Agriculture. Tuber survey."

"Those things hurt cars?"

"No. Goes right through metal. Picks up different kinds of plants. Carrots and things."

"What kind of things?" asked Willie the Plumber.

"Oh, I don't know. Carrots. Turnips. Poppies, I guess."

"Poppies? You mean them red things on veterans' day."

"Leave me alone," the man said.

"I'm just asking friendly questions. If you want to find out about carrots and turnips, why don't you go to the vegetable market?"

"Don't ask me, fella. It's the government."

Willie nodded and warned the man that the thing he was using better not hurt his Eldorado or the man would be "sucking on a lead pipe."

Then Willie the Plumber steered himself carefully back to his car, filing away the survey of carrots, turnips and poppies as a little fact of life he would not share with anyone until he saw a profit in it.

CHAPTER ELEVEN

It was really getting good now.

There was no way out of it.

Vance Masterman simply had to tell Loretta that he could not marry her because she was his daughter. That would free her to turn in Professor Singbar Ramkwat as the thief of the lymph node cure and then Loretta could marry Bart Henderson and he would continue his research work. Not even Claire Wentworth, Loretta's mother, could be dissatisfied with that, particularly since it gave her a clear field to Dr. Bruce Barton.

But it all hinged on Vance Masterman telling Loretta. In just minutes it had to happen and Chiun was more than happy. Happiness, he demonstrated by rocking slightly back and forth while sitting in his full lotus position on the floor of their East Side apartment. When he was really overjoyed, sometimes he hummed. Today, Chiun was rocking and humming. Ecstasy.

He turned up the volume on the television set so as not to miss a word and then he waited for the solution to the problems of an entire community.

Braaaawk.

It was the door bell.

Whoever it was would simply have to wait. There were only about eight minutes left in the show anyway. Chiun could tell.

Braaaaaaaaaaaaawk.

This time, the loud insistent squawk of the door bell threatened to overwhelm the music, violins and organs, sobbing from the television set.

Let him wait.

Of course, one should never let a person wait at a front door. That was rudeness and Orientals did not believe in rudeness. On the other hand, eighty-year-old Koreans who had attained peace with themselves, did not get up and walk away from the great moment of a show that they had watched for seven years to coax to this point. Politeness or self-contentment?

Courtesy was a duty and in his eight decades on the planet, Chiun had never shirked his duty. He was ready to shirk now, ready to sit Vance Masterman through right until the end and if someone waited in the hall until his feet grew roots through the carpet, that was too bad. People should not come visiting when good shows are on.

The impasse, fortunately, was resolved by up organ music, slow dissolve, momentary silence and then the appearance on screen of a lady plumber belly-laughing the stains out of sinks in New York City.

Chiun jumped to his feet and began running. Out of the living room, through the dining room, down the hallway, his long brocaded white robe swirling about his ankles.

Braaaaaaaaaaaaaaaaaaaa aaaaaawk.

Chiun reached up and unlocked the door. Then he unlocked the safety dead bolt. Then he went to remove the safety chain, all of which he had been assured were absolutely necessary to keep fastened at all times if one wished to remain alive in New York City for the better part of an afternoon.

But the safety chain was stuck and did not pull off its slide. So Chiun held the chain in his left hand and with a silent expulsion of air, brought his right fingertips down against the offending chain, searing one link as if it had been sliced by a bolt cutter.

Then Chiun turned the doorknob, pulled the door open fractionally, turned and was racing back down the hall, through the dining room, into the living room and back into his lotus position.

Organ music up, then fade in and enter Vance Masterman. "Dear, I have something to tell you. . . ."

In the hallway, Johnny the Duck, Vinnie O'Boyle and Pops Smith, saw the door swing open slightly. They looked at each other with suspicion and Johnny the Duck reached into the shoulder holster under his left armpit and removed a .45 caliber pistol. He touched the door tentatively with his left hand, then waited until the door swung all the way back, stopping with a soft thud against the wall. No one behind it.

The three men stepped inside, Johnny the Duck first as befitted his rank, then O'Boyle, followed by Pops Smith, a tall, shuffling, black man whose eternal grin was relieved only slightly by a scar that furrowed down his face from alongside his right eye to the point of his chin.

Pops had gotten it when he tried to hold out and continue running his small independent numbers operation in the face of a stated desire by the Mafia that it take over Pops' numbers. For a consideration, of course, since it simply was not good business procedure to allow him to pay winners higher odds than the Mafia did, because, after all, there was such a thing as unfair competition and how could man survive in such a dog-eat-dog world. They made this point clear to Pops by slashing his face with a linoleum knife and warning him that the next time it would be his genitals.

Pops, who had been a big fish in a small pond, opted to become a fully-equipped, if small fish, in the Mafia's big gambling pond. While he still sometimes harbored suspicions that the Mafia was not truly concerned with entrepreneurship among minorities and was even at times bigoted, he did not express those opinions to anyone, especially not to Gaetano Gasso, who had sent him here today.

Pops looked anxiously now over the shoulders of Johnny the Duck and Vinnie O'Boyle. The long carpeted hall was empty. Funny they had heard or seen no one at the door.

The Duck nodded to Pops who fastened the two locks that still worked. Pops shook his head at the sight of the broken chain lock. A good way to get yourself killed in New York City, letting maintenance go that way.

Cautiously, the three men walked slowly down the hall, in sort of an ethnic pecking order in the Mafia: Johnny the Duck first, followed by the Irishman O'Boyle, followed by the black Pops Smith. Despite their best efforts, their feet made small scuffing noises on the carpet and the Duck removed the safety on his gun. Up ahead, they could hear voices. Funny, O'Boyle thought, that fifty bucks to the doorman told them that the dink was here alone.

Softly now into the dining room. The voices were louder now and O'Boyle took out his gun too, a .38 caliber police special with burned-off serial numbers.

The dining room opened into the living room through a large archway. They smiled at each other in relief. The voices came from the television set and in front of it, squatting on the floor, enraptured by the pale gray image in the bright sunlit room, sat the dink, his back to them.

"There's nothing you have to tell me that I want to hear," came a woman's voice from the television. The dink was rocking and humming.

Johnny the Duck chuckled and put his gun back into his shoulder holster. So did Vinnie O'Boyle. They noticed that Pops had not taken out his gun and that annoyed the other two, because he would be sure to tell Gasso how stupid both of them had looked with their guns aimed at the back of the aged, tiny Oriental who could hurt nothing more than his eyes if he sat too close to the set. And Gasso would needle them about it. Maybe for weeks, maybe for months, maybe forever.

And there was nothing you could do about Gasso's needling except take it. Maybe for weeks, maybe for months, maybe forever.

They stepped into the parquet-floored living room, their metal cleated heels making sharp clicks on the highly polished wood.

"Hey, you," Johnny the Duck called at the back of the brocaded, white robe. It kept rocking. Its occupant kept humming. Johnny the Duck walked around in front of Chiun and looked down into the placid Oriental face. A peaceful-looking old man.

107

"Yeah, you," Johnny the Duck said. "We want to talk with you."

In musical English, Chiun said, "My house is your house. Make yourself at home. I will be with you soon," and he moved his head slightly to see around the right leg of Johnny the Duck.

The Duck looked at the other two men who still stood near the doorway behind Chiun and he shrugged. They grinned and shrugged back.

"But I must tell you," Vance Masterman's voice pleaded from the television. "I have borne this secret in silence for these many years and. . . ."

"The gook wants to watch his television show," Johnny the Duck said. "Maybe we ought to let him."

"Why not?" O'Boyle agreed and the Duck moved out of Chiun's way.

There were two things Pops Smith didn't like. First was calling the old man a gook and a dink. He couldn't help where he was born or what his color was.

Pops mentioned this to O'Boyle and the Duck. "No need to make fun of the old man. He just old, is all."

Chiun heard the voice and the words. For that, Pops had earned himself a gift—the gift of dying last.

Unfortunately, Pop lost all claim to the gift later when he took action on the second thing he didn't like.

"What makes you think I would believe anything you say?" the woman's voice whined from the television.

Chiun continued to hum, but his rocking became more rhythmical, as if he were impatiently urging the

108

players on. Tell her, he said to himself. Just tell her, *I am your father.*

Chiun would have done it. Remo would have done it. Any man would have done it. But now the picture was fading and the organ music was rising and Vance Masterman still had not told her. Chiun sighed, a deep anguished sigh. At times, Vance Masterman was a very imperfect human being.

If only he were more like the lady plumber who now appeared on the screen—racing in front of the camera, braying her message, demonstrating her wares and then leaving.

Ah, but Vance Masterman had had a difficult life and men reacted differently to adversity. He had once told that to Remo at a training session.

They had sat on the gymnasium floor at Folcroft Sanatorium and Chiun had looked at Remo's face. At first, he had despaired of ever making anything of this hard-faced, wisecracking young man. But as time went on and the legend grew, that had changed and Chiun felt for him, first kindness, then respect, then almost love, and he had shared with him a secret.

"In the world, Remo, you will find that men will do what men must do. Learn to anticipate men and you learn to control men. Learn also not to be anticipated. Learn to be like the wind that blows from all sides; then men will look at you and never know what window of their soul to close."

Chiun arose in one motion from his full lotus and stood up, slightly annoyed at himself for not realizing that Vance Masterman would have trouble telling his terrible secret.

He turned to his three guests. The one who had

stood in front of him: he had had to because it was the way for an inferior man to demonstrate superiority. And the one who had agreed that Chiun should watch his television. He also had had to, because he was a stupid man, and being agreeable made it unnecessary to attempt to think one's way through to a decision. And the third man, the black man who had raised his voice in protest of the verbal abuse of Chiun. Well, that—too—was preordained. He defended himself by defending Chiun.

Chiun would have to tell Remo about these very interesting men. Remo was interested these days in why people did things.

Chiun smiled and folded his hands inside the large, flowing sleeves of his brocaded white robe.

"Gentlemen?" he said. It was a question.

"You finished watching that soap opera?" Johnny the Duck asked.

"Yes. For the time being. There will be commercials now and five minutes of news before the next program appears. We may talk." He waved them graciously to seats. They remained standing.

"We didn't come to talk, dink," O'Boyle said. "We came to hear talk."

"The speech therapist is on the next floor," Chiun said.

"Listen, Mr. Moto, you just go along with what we say and you ain't going to get hurt," Johnny the Duck said.

"This frail old specter will remember you with nothing but gratitude," Chiun said.

The Duck nodded to O'Boyle. "Keep an eye on him. Make sure he don't run." Then he walked to-

110

ward the telephone to call a number in Hudson, a number he had never called before.

* * *

From his position on the floor under the fourteen-foot long mahogany table in Mayor Craig Hansen's office, Remo could not reach the telephone. From her position under Remo, neither could Cynthia Hansen, the mayor's daughter.

"Let it ring," Remo said.

"I can't let it ring," she said, placing the words in his ear along with the tip of her tongue. "I'm a public servant." She accented her words by plunging her naked pelvis against Remo's naked body.

"Forget about servicing the public. Service the private," Remo said and returned the stroke with interest.

"When I was told that working in city hall was just screwing the public, I never thought I'd be doing it one at a time," she said, and reached down between them and grabbed Remo. "Now unplug, will you?" she said squeezing slightly to make her point.

"Government is no career for weaklings," Remo sighed. He slowly, lovingly withdrew and rolled off her. Cynthia Hansen rolled out from under the table and padded naked across the seventy-two dollar a yard carpet, bought without public bidding, to the telephone. She picked it up as she sat back in the tan leather chair, $627 without bidding, put her long legs up on the desk and looked down at her left nipple which was still rigid with excitement.

"Mayor Hansen's office," she said, "May I help you?" squeezing her nipple between the index and middle fingers of her right hand.

111

She listened for a moment, then held out the phone with a shrug. "It's for you," she said in surprise, then shrugged again.

Remo groaned to himself, then still erect, got to his feet and walked around the desk, until he was between the desk and Cynthia Hansen. She dropped her legs to let him reach the telephone, but then put her legs back up onto the desk trapping Remo in the middle.

Remo picked up the telephone and propped it on his shoulder. "It's your dime," he said, and using both hands, he lifted Cynthia's knees slightly, then tilted the tan leather chair back so that her pelvis was tipped up toward him. He slowly leaned forward toward her.

"Listen, Barry," the voice came over the phone. "We know what you're doing."

Remo was in and he started to stroke gently, forward and back. "Five bucks says you don't," he told the voice.

"Yeah?" said Johnny the Duck.

"Yeah," said Remo.

"Yeah? Well, anyway we know everything about you, except who made you come."

"You wouldn't believe me if I told you," Remo said, pumping harder now. "And after a couple of years, too." He leaned forward and with his hands began to manipulate Cynthia's breasts.

"Yeah? Well, we got the dink. What d'ya think about that?"

"Tell him to make you some chop suey. He's really good at it, but watch the soy sauce. He's got a tendency to use too much. . .too. . .much!," Remo said and then it was over

"Hey, Barry. You all right?" Johnny the Duck wondered over the phone.

"Yeah. I'm fine now," Remo said, lying there heavily against Cynthia Hansen, waiting for the pulsating throb to cease.

"Well, if you ever want to see the dink again, you better talk."

"What do you want me to say?"

"Somebody's going to give you the password. Butterflies. When that someone does, you tell him everything you know. What you're doing here and who sent you and all. Otherwise, you'll never see the dink again."

Remo pulled out and sat his bare butt on the glass panel that topped the desk.

"Listen, fella. How do I know you've got him?"

"We got him. We don't kid around."

"I want to talk to him," Remo said. "How do I know you haven't killed him already?"

Silence for a moment, then Johnny the Duck said, "Okay. Here he is. But no funny business." Then off the phone, he called, "Hey, dink. Your boss wants to talk to you."

The accented voice that came next onto the line was Chiun's and Remo, looking down at Cynthia Hansen, still hot, still wanting, in front of him had a difficult decision to make.

"Listen, Chiun. Will they all fit in the freezer?

"Ah, balls. Okay, stick them in the bathtub. Pack them in ice or something."

Then Johnny the Duck was back on the line. "That's enough. See, wise guy, we got him. Now it's up to you if he lives or not. Remember. It'll be a person what says butterflies."

"Yeah, sure, pal. Anything you say. Do me just one favor, will you? Tell the old guy to use plenty of ice and to turn up the air conditioner."

"What?" asked Johnny the Duck.

"Look," Remo said. "I'll do anything you want. But just do this one thing for me, huh? Tell him I said to use plenty of ice and to turn up the air conditioner. Okay? Okay. Thanks, pal. You'll never regret it."

He hung up the phone. Cynthia Hansen lay with her eyes closed, her nipples at attention, her legs still framing him against the desk.

"Now, where was I?" he said.

"You can start anywhere," she said.

Johnny the Duck hung up the telephone, a look of puzzlement on his face. The commercials were over, along with the news; the organ interlude was over; and Lawrence Walters, psychiatrist, was on, preparing to unravel the tortured mind of Beverly Ransom, who was racked with guilt because she felt herself the cause of the death of her own daughter in a train accident, since she had insisted upon sending the girl to summer camp, and until she was cured, she could never again be a real wife to Royal Ransom, millionaire banker and chief financial backer of Dr. Lawrence Walters' street-level, store-front psychiatric clinic. Chiun was again seated in front of the television set, staring fixedly at the washed-out grayed picture, picking the images out of a grayness which was accented by the sunshine which fell across the dusty screen.

The Duck looked at Chiun. "Listen, dink."

Chiun held up a hand to forestall more talk.

"I'm talking to you," Johnny the Duck said. Chiun

114

ignored him. Pops Smith found he did not like that. It was all right to be Oriental and old, but they were here on no laughing matter and they deserved respect.

Johnny the Duck nodded to Pops Smith who got up off a soft overstuffed chair and walked around in front of Chiun. "Sorry, old man, but we're not fooling around," he said and hit the button that turned the television off. That cost him the favor he had earned earlier.

Chiun's concentration was broken and he rose slowly, pathetically small and frail, and he looked around more in sorrow than in anger.

The Duck said, "I don't know what the hell he's talking about, but your boss said use plenty of ice and turn up the air conditioner."

"Why did you turn off my television show?" Chiun asked.

"Cause we got to wait here for a phone call and we ain't gonna wait and listen to all that stupidness," Johnny the Duck said.

If Pops Smith had not turned off the television set, he would have had something to think about, something to make him wonder if just one poor, black man could have done more with his numbers business than fold before the power and might of the Mafia. Pops Smith might have had a chance to think that one man, one poor, insignificant man, could be pretty powerful after all and might be able to win, even against long odds.

But Pops Smith had been the instrument that interrupted the saga of Dr. Lawrence Walters and his never-ending battle against mankind's age-old problems of superstition, ignorance and mental illness. And so

115

Pops' skull was shattered first and he never had the chance to see Johnny the Duck somehow lifted off his feet and propelled across the room into the bewildered face of Vinnie O'Boyle, and Pops never got the opportunity to hear their temple bones give under the pressure of just two index fingers, never had the chance to think to himself that he didn't really have to surrender his business to the Mafia because perhaps it wasn't that powerful after all.

In death, he could see or hear or think of none of those things. He just lay on the floor, his eyes open but unseeing, as the television slowly brightened back on as Dr. Lawrence Walters said that guilt and repressed hostility were most destructive to the human psyche.

Forty-five minutes later, the man—known as Remo Barry—and Cynthia Hansen decided they were done for the day.

"What was the phone call about?" she asked as she picked up her see-through blouse.

"Put on your skirt first," Remo said, sitting back naked in the mayor's tan leather chair, looking out over a street filled with happy Puerto Ricans, happy luncheonettes and happy record stores. "I've always been a tit man."

"Don't be indelicate," she said. "The phone call?"

"Oh. Some of your town's drug business hoodlums were holding my servant prisoner. They said they were going to kill him if I didn't spill my guts to whoever told me the password."

"Butterflies," said Cynthia Hansen.

"Yeah, that's right," Remo said. "Eavesdropper."

"Well, what about your servant? Aren't you worried?"

"Only about the air conditioning. I know he won't forget the ice, but he doesn't like the apartment too cool, so he might forget the air conditioning."

"What the hell are you talking about?" Cynthia Hansen said as she finished buttoning her skirt up the front, her fine young breasts trembling with the motion. "He might be dead or being tortured."

Remo looked at the clock on the mirrored mantel. "It's two o'clock. 'Edge of Life' just went off. Maybe I'd better call him." He picked up the phone and dialed.

He waited a few moments, then smiled. "Chiun? Yeah, how's it going? Did Vance Masterman finally work that thing out today?

"Oh, that's too bad. I'm really sorry for you. Listen, I was thinking that lobster might be good tonight. Yeah. You know how you make it, with the wine sauce. Okay. Okay. And Chiun," he added importantly, "don't forget the air conditioning."

Remo hung up. "Boy, I'm glad you made me call. He forgot the air conditioner."

Cynthia Hansen just stared as she buttoned up her see-through blouse.

CHAPTER TWELVE

But Remo did not eat dinner at home.

Cynthia Hansen offered to drive him to the subway, but as they drove along in her black city-issued Chevrolet, he stared at her long bare legs expertly working the brake and accelerator, and then looked up and realized she had turned the rear-view mirror so she could watch him. By the time they had reached the subway station in Hudson Square, they were hungry for each other again and they decided to have dinner together at her apartment.

Cynthia Hansen lived alone in a six-room apartment on the top floor of an eight-story apartment building that was one of the city's best. It still had a doorman and it had an elevator that worked, which was rare in Hudson, and the garbage had been allowed to lay uncollected in the cellar only once—until Cynthia Hansen had unleashed a flood of city inspectors on the property, papering everyone with summonses, until the owner who lived in Great Neck decided to do something about the garbage.

But the rooms were maze-like, seemingly unconnected, as if they were designed by a drunken architect, and in his first five minutes in the apartment,

Remo made three wrong turns looking for the bathroom.

Cynthia's refrigerator was well-stocked, but they decided to dine on salami and cheese. Remo would not let her slice either with a knife, but instead tore off hunks for both of them.

And Remo had her in the kitchen while she was putting food onto a tray; he had her on the parquet floor of the living room which was cold against her back and his knees among the salami skins and cheese rinds; then he had her in the shower where they lovingly lathered each other's bodies and used each other as washclothes. From kitchen to living room to shower, it was one of the great displays of coitus interruptus and then Remo made it non-interruptus as he finished shagging her on the hard, unyielding mattress of the four poster bed in her enormous bedroom, with the blue velvet-striped wallpaper on one wall.

Afterwards, they lay naked, side by side, on top of the blue velvet spread and Remo decided that since he seemed intent on screwing his brains out, he might as well bust training all the way, so he joined Cynthia Hansen in a cigarette and made a mental note to buy spearmint gum on the way back to New York so Chiun would not smell the smoke on his breath.

"Ever think about going into government?" Cynthia Hansen said to him, and blew smoke rings toward the ceiling, then handed the cigarette across her body to Remo.

"Ever since I've met you, I've done nothing but go into government," Remo said

"I think I could find something good for you," she said. "What do you make at that stupid magazine anyway?"

"Good year, I might do eight, nine thousand."

"I can get you eighteen and you don't even have to show up."

"To be the royal stud?"

"To work for me. On whatever I ask you to do."

"Sorry. I don't believe in working for women. It's degrading."

"You're a male chauvinist pig," Cynthia Hansen said. "I really wish you'd think about it. There's not much future in what you're doing now."

"Which is?"

"Which appears to be walking around, insulting people, causing trouble and getting people very upset."

"It's my nature," Remo said, and tried to blow a smoke ring but failed abysmally. Annoyed, he stubbed out the cigarette in an ashtray on an end table next to the bed, then, absently, picked up a small photo in a golden gilt frame.

"Your mother" Remo asked, holding the picture of a smiling couple up in front of Cynthia.

"Yes. And my father."

"She's a good looking woman. You've got her face," he said, and he really meant it because Mayor Craig Hansen, the other person in the picture, was handsome, insipid and characterless. His face had all the distinction of a phonograph record.

"I know," Cynthia said. "People always tell me I look like my mother."

Remo put the picture back. She lit another cigarette, they smoked it and she again offered him a job at City Hall. "Do you think you can buy me off, you insidious heroin peddler, you?" he asked, and then he was getting dressed, because it was dark outside and it was time to go back to see Chiun. Cynthia stayed him, offering him a job for a third time which he refused for a third time. Then he held her bare butt in his hands, and told her he would see her tomorrow, and Cynthia Hansen allowed herself to fear that he would never see her or anyone else again.

But she was wrong.

Gaetano Gasso's silver crochet needle flashed back and forth. He stared intently at the doily he was working on. He was trying a new stitch and it was difficult to pick up the correct thread each time. He had done it wrong three times now and he was beginning to lose his temper. And when Gaetano Gasso lost his temper, people had reason to worry.

He sat alone at a bare desk in the corner of a mammoth warehouse—a warehouse that was stark empty except for one automobile. It was Gasso's automobile, a 1968 Chevrolet sedan that once was a police car. He had purchased it at an auction for city cars and got it for $5 when the junk dealers who normally bought such cars for $25 all developed serious cases of lockjaw. For another $10 he had had it tuned up at a good garage he knew on Paterson Plankroad in Secaucus; for $10 he had two kids paint it yellow; and for 25 bucks he had himself good dependable wheels. It was good to have a friend in city hall.

It was no use. He could not concentrate on the doily. It was that writer. That smart-ass writer. Well, tonight he would take care of that smart-ass writer, and he allowed himself a smile at the prospect. First he would work him over, find out what he was really doing in town and what had happened to The Duck and O'Boyle and Pops, then he would kill him. He looked forward to the prospect and he rubbed his big hands together. Then he could get that stitch right. Crocheting took concentration. That Remo Barry would pay the price for disturbing Gaetano Gasso's concentration.

A steel door at the front of the warehouse opened and Willie the Plumber Palumbo stuck his head in reluctantly and called, "Mister Gasso? Mister Gasso?"

Gasso stood up behind the desk in the corner. The Plumber saw him and said loudly, "We got him for you, Mr. Gasso. We got him." Then Willie the Plumber walked into the warehouse, followed by a medium-tall, medium-husky stranger, who was followed by Steve Lillisio who had a gun poked into the stranger's back.

Willie the Plumber let the two men walk in front of him, locked the door behind them, then hurried to get back in front of the procession. He smiled as he neared Gasso, who had moved alongside the desk, and hoped to coax a smile in return. Nothing.

— "We got him, Mr. Gasso. We got him. Real easy. Just picked him right up off the street. We got him for you."

Gasso ignored him. Willie coughed. Something came up into his mouth, but he wasn't sure of Mr. Gasso's position on spitting so he swallowed it.

Gasso was looking at the man in the middle. Remo Barry. He didn't look like enough to cause all this trouble. Remo Barry, meanwhile, was looking around him at the warehouse, all around—at the ceilings, at the floors, at the walls. Finally he turned his head to Gasso.

"How you want to die?" Gasso asked.

"What do I want to die for? But I'll tell you, you keep sneaking up on me like that and I'll die of shock. You're enough to scare somebody to death. How do you get that hair to grow all over you? Some kind of plant food, right? Huh?"

Willie the Plumber Palumbo and Steve Lillisio stood there silently. It was not nice to talk that way to Mr. Gasso. They hoped he would tell them to go. They did not want to be there to see what was going to happen to this writer.

The writer was still talking. "Does the Museum of Natural History know you're here? I mean, it's just not right to keep Margaret Mead out of this. The last time anybody found something like you, it was in a cave. How come you don't have hair on your teeth? I saw something in a display case once that looked like you and I would have sworn it had hair on its teeth."

Mr. Gasso was going to talk. His mouth was moving and Willie the Plumber Palumbo hoped that he would say, "Okay, Willie the Plumber. Go home. You did a good job, now go home and leave me alone with this creep." But Mr. Gasso talked to the writer instead. "I asked you how you want to die?"

Remo looked down at the desk and saw the crocheting. "Hey, look," he said, "crocheting." He picked up the needle and the thread. "That's pretty good. Really, fella, that's pretty good. You keep practicing and pretty soon they'll be able to sell them. It's good for people like you to make a buck. Makes you feel worthwhile, doesn't it? Not like you're a burden on someone."

He leaned forward toward Gasso. "Come on," he whispered. "You can tell me. How do you get all that hair to grow? I won't tell anybody. It's not a wig, is it? I mean a body-sized wig is too much. Maybe some kind of astro-turf. Does it hurt your knees when you run? Do you have knees? It's hard to tell. I mean, I can see you don't have any wrists, but I can't see your knees. If you have knees."

He turned back to Willie the Plumber. "C'mon, you probably know. Does this thing have knees? It's important, so think carefully before you answer. If it doesn't have any knees, it might be a whole new species. We might make a buck. Imagine, finding a whole new species."

Of all the things Willie did not want, the thing he did not want most was to be drawn into this lunatic's conversation. Among the other things he did not want was to show anything that looked like a smile. He did not want to even look as if he had been listening.

So his mind worked fast and finally he said, "Just shut your face. Mr. Gasso asked you a question."

"Question? Oh yeah, how do I want to die?" Remo turned and looked at Gasso. "Well, guns kind of take the fun out of it and you might get disfigured if we used knives. And I wouldn't want that to happen, at least not until the museum gets its people over here to look at you."

Remo shrugged. "Anything you want's all right with me. How about clubs? Is your species using clubs yet?"

Willie the Plumber watched. Mr. Gasso was about to speak. Maybe he was about to send Willie the Plumber away. Gasso's mouth moved, but again he addressed his words to Remo Barry. "Last guy talked like that I pulled his arms out. He didn't make no more jokes after that."

"Guess not," Remo said.

"But I got something better for you."

"Oh? I wonder what it could be?" Remo snapped his fingers. "I know. You're going to give me a doily. All for myself. Hey, fella, that's really nice of you too. I know how long it takes you people to do a thing like this, trying to coordinate your fingers and all, and I want you to know I really appreciate it."
— Gasso spoke again. "Willie the Plumber, you can go. You too, Lillisio." To Willie, he said, "Come back in the morning, so you can pick up what's left of him and get rid of it someplace."

He stopped momentarily, then asked, "You checked him for a gun?"

"Yes, Mr. Gasso," Willie the Plumber said. "He ain't carrying."

"Okay. Get out of here now. This comedian's gonna start talking and he's gonna tell me who sent him."

Willie the Plumber and Lillisio set a new world's record for trans-warehouse flight. When the door clicked closed behind them, Gasso reached into his pocket and pulled out a brass key. "This unlocks the door. If you can take it off me, you win. You can go." He put the key back in his pocket.

Remo said, "I'm not going to take it off you. You're going to give it to me."

"Why?" Gasso asked.

"So that I'll stop the pain."

Gasso lunged. His tree trunk arms encircled Remo around the chest, under Remo's arms.

"First, I'm going to take some of the snot out of you, buddy," Gasso grunted. "Then I'm going to peel

125

your skin like an orange." He locked his hands behind Remo and squeezed. He gave it the hundred per cent squeeze, guaranteed to crack ribs and bring on unconsciousness.

Remo reached behind him with his hands and encircled the parts of Gasso's arms that would, on a normal person, be wrists. He concentrated on his hands and blanked his mind so that nothing existed for him but his hands and he remembered one of Chiun's innumerable chants, "I am created Shiva, the destroyer; death, the shatterer of worlds," then he began to pull Gasso's arms apart.

Gasso's fingers felt slippery and then he felt the fingers began to slide. One hand gave up its hold on the other and his hands separated. It had never happened before. He roared and tried to close his arms again, but this punk—this Barry—had him and slowly, like a giant machine, he was pulling Gasso's arms apart. Then Gasso's arms were at his sides, then extended out by his shoulders and this Remo punk was smiling at him and still pressuring. Then Gasso felt his shoulder muscles begin to give. They were tearing and the arms were pulling out of the sockets. The pain was excruciating and Gasso screamed, a blood-curdling scream that resounded through the empty warehouse and then echoed off the ceiling and the walls, fed on its own intensity and carried even to outdoors, where Willie the Plumber Palumbo was just closing the door of his Eldorado behind him.

Willie the Plumber stopped for a moment when he heard the scream, then closed the door. Willie was careful to say the correct thing because he did not know if Lillisio might be the kind of guy to carry stories back. So he said, "I feel sorry for the poor bas-

126

tard. But he shouldn't oughta made fun of Mr. Gasso."

And Willie drove away quickly. He did not want to hear more. He had been told to come back in the morning to dispose of what was left and his stomach was churning at the thought of what that would look like.

Poor Remo Barry.

CHAPTER THIRTEEN

There are are two hundred six bones in the human body. It was the kind of fact that Don Dominic Verillio remembered, and it was in large measure responsible for the reputation he had among his Mafia underlings for erudition and culture.

Don Dominic also felt he had a logical mind. Since there were two hundred six bones in the human body and since Gaetano Gasso was—despite his appearance—a human being, it therefore followed that Gaetano Gasso had two hundred six bones in his body also.

And every one of them was broken.

Don Dominic Varillio was not a religious man. It is true that he went to church every Sunday and on every holy day of obligation, but he went as a business investment. As a community leader, he must lead a community leader's life. He must be God-fearing and religious. In his true business as *Capo Mafioso,* the knowledge among his troops that he was a religious man could often compensate for some particular ghastly thing that Verillio, as the leader of leaders, must do or order done.

So he was not really a religious man. But he now

crossed himself as he looked down upon the body of what was once Gaetano Gasso.

The body that only fifteen hours earlier had been a solid lump of muscle now looked like jello slowly melting inside an ill-fitting man-shaped sausage casing. It had been pulverized into a bag of mush.

The arms were flung out wildly and where arms normally transcribed only angles, Gasso's arms were bent into true curves, which was only possible because the bones that normally lent arms their rigidity, had been broken. And broken. And broken again.

And so had the legs and the ribs and the head. But that by itself was not enough to make Don Dominic Verillio bless himself and make the sign of the cross.

Growing out of the center of Gasso's forehead like a horrible antenna was a silver crochet hook, driven through the bone, into the brain, by some force that Don Dominic Verillio could not imagine. But that by itself was not enough to make Don Dominic Verillio bless himself.

What made Verillio utter a silent prayer, to whatever god might be out there who was still unattached and could fight on his side, was this:

Gaetano Gasso was naked. A white doily he had been crocheting had been dropped carefully over his private parts. Ordinarily, its white color would have stood out starkly against the black hair that coated Gasso's body from head to toe. But it did not now because Gasso's hair was no longer black. The hair on his head, and on his shoulders and chest and stomach and legs and feet and arms was white. Snow white.

And for that, Don Dominic Verillio blessed himself. No one should have to die that way. Not even Gaetano Gasso who specialized in terrible deaths.

Next to Verillio stood Willie the Plumber Palumbo, who had discovered the body that morning and had telephoned Verillio to come to the warehouse. Willie the Plumber was muttering, and Verillio saw that he was fingering a rosary and saying his beads.

He started to interrupt, to tell Willie the Plumber to stop, and then he checked himself. Gasso. And no word from the three men sent yesterday to Remo Barry's apartment to force information from the old Chinaman.

What were they up against? Maybe Willie was right to pray.

Don Dominic Verillio thought about that as he drove his Lincoln Continental back to the center of town where his office was located in the Chamber of Commerce building.

He was thinking about it as he drove past St. Alexander's Church, an old Catholic church, whose architect seemed to be trying to tell everyone something by building a Byzantine temple.

When he saw a meter, Verillio pulled over to the curb and carefully parked his car. He put 10 cents in the meter, then walked back to the church. It was cool inside, a blessed change from the heat that pummeled the city, even this early in the morning. Don Dominic Verillio slid into a pew at the very back of the church and kneeled down and stared at the altar which he had purchased for St. Alexander's Church in memory of his mother.

Old Pietro's half-witted daughter had warned him. And was she not often right? Did she not say he would marry and had she not said his wife would die. Had she not known about the daughter no one else knew about? And now, she had said he was going

130

againts a god. Had he? Was there such a thing as Shiva the destroyer?

He thought of Gasso, white haired and pulp, lying on the floor of the warehouse and his lips began to move in the unthinking words of childhood.

"Our father, Who art in heaven, hallowed be. . . ." He stared at the altar, his altar, and he hoped that the real God would remember it. He tried to concentrate on the image of Christ there, but his eyes went blank and all he could see was Gasso; then the faces of those other three men who had disappeared yesterday.

" . . . Thy will be done, on earth. . . ." Thy will? Whose will? Verillio thought of another face, the face of that writer, Remo Barry, smiling and hardfaced. Even if he is a god, he isn't my God, and it isn't right for him to be here. What kind of god can he be anyway? Old ladies' superstition.

But there was Gasso.

" . . . Our daily bread and lead us not. . . ."

Verillio fixed his eyes on the crucifix behind his altar. Jesus, you hear me now. *I may not be the best, but what have you got that's better? The altar. The summer camp. The carpeting in the convent. There's more, Jesus, where that came from. More. That's if things keep going. But there won't be anything, Lord, if this new guy takes over. If he gets everybody believing that god stuff. There won't be anything then for you, Lord.*

" . . .But deliver us from evil. . . ."

Don Dominic Verillio looked at the crucifix, waiting for a sign that his bargain had been accepted, but he saw none.

In the rear of the church, the Rev. F. H. Maguire

131

stood, looking over his new church. He had been a
curate in four churches now, each more impressive
than the next and this one was magnificent. It was
strange. The outside world had a view of Hudson as
if it were peopled by Mafia thugs, crooks and gam-
blers. It was unfair, Father Maguire thought.

The people of Hudson built beautiful churches and
they filled them on Sundays and holy days. Until anything was proven differently, Father Maguire was
willing to take them as they came. Like that man in
the last row over there. Obviously, a man of some
standing in the community. And probably an every-
day church goer. Father Maguire tried to read the
man by looking at him. Solid, stable, deeply religious
—but worried. Yes, there was worry in the crinkle of
the eyes. And his lips were moving, but not in ritu-
alistic prayers. He was talking directly to God, and
worried men did that most often.

*We got a deal, Jesus, or not? You just going to
give up and let somebody else move in, masquerading
as you? It matters, you know. If you aren't the man,
then a lot of money goes somewhere else. A lot of
widows and orphans and poor people are going to be
hurt. Because of you. Make up your mind, Jesus. I
don't have all day.*

Father Maguire shook his head as he watched the
man in the rear pew. His lips were moving now and
despite the coolness of the church, sweat was running
down his face. He was agitated. Obviously arguing
with God. It could be dangerous to the man's faith
and the man's soul if he were allowed to go on.

The Rev. F. H. Maguire was one of God's acti-
vists. He believed in CYO newspapers, bowling
leagues and theater parties—but only as a means to

an end, not an end in themselves. The end was the tortured souls of tortured people, like this fine looking man in the last pew.

Father Maguire walked over, and slid into the pew next to Verillio, folded his hands and put them on the back of the seat in front of him. When Verillio looked at him, he smiled, leaned toward him and whispered, "Do not despair, sir. Though he moves in strange ways, through strange instruments, God accomplishes God's work. It is not for us to know how. It is not for us to understand all the means. It is enough for us to know that whoever does God's work stands with Christ, in triumph through eternity, no matter what forces are arrayed against him.

"The good man will crush the evil," Father Maguire said, and he smiled.

Verillio stared at him. Father Maguire kept smiling, so Verillio rose to his feet, then pushed past the priest and out into the aisle. He walked rapidly. It turned into a run, out across the back and down the broad front steps of the church.

Don Dominic Verillio prided himself on never having been stupid. And as he drove to his office now, he told himself that again. When times changed, Don Dominic changed with them. When it was time to strike, he had struck. But now it was time to flee. He would flee.

He tapped his foot impatiently as he rode up in the uncrowded elevator to his suite of offices in the Chamber of Commerce building, and he tried to seem unconcerned and pleasant as he said good morning to his secretary.

"I'll take no calls for awhile," he told her. Inside his inner office, he pulled back a painting on the wall.

133

It was one of Eve Flynn's. That was one of the reasons to flee and not to die because Eve Flynn gave a vision of life that was worth living for, so he dialed three numbers on a combination safe and opened the safe. But inside there was just another combination safe. Before touching that dial he went to his desk and pressed a switch which cut the electrical power to the safe, then went back to dial the numbers that opened it.

He opened his empty attaché case and began carefully, neatly taking the contents of the safe out and putting them in the attaché case. There were papers and money. The papers were more important because they told whom Verillio took his orders from, and that person must be protected at any cost. At all costs. Even if it came to running up against this Shiva.

The money. Well, handy money was handy money, even though he could get his hands on millions. It was always a good idea to have some walking-around money, Verillio thought, as he pulled out the $10,000 stacks and dropped them into his attaché case.

Then he closed the safe and began to look through his top desk drawer when his secretary opened the door, smiling.

"Mister Verillio. It's the Shiva fellow again. Destroyer of Worlds. Heh, heh. He says it's important."

Verillio sank back into his leather seat. "Ask him to wait a minute, please. I'll be right with him."

She closed the door and Verillio pulled the papers from his attaché case and dropped them into a shredder basket under the desk. He would not find out from Verillio. Don Dominic would protect the brains. The papers he had taken from the safe were all shredded now, whirred up under the desk. Verillio felt relief.

From his top right hand desk drawer, he took a .38 caliber pistol and spun the cylinder, checking. It was loaded. He felt its cold weight in his hand and smiled to himself. How long had it been since he had handled a gun? How long that he had been on top of the heap and others used the guns? Somehow, it felt like an old friend, sitting there in his hand, heavy and lethal.

It had done his work many times before. It would do it now. He tried to remember how many he had killed before, but the number escaped him since it was no longer part of his past. He was like the hooker movie star who forgot the whorehouse. Just forget it. He forgot the violence. But it had always been there. He cocked the pistol now, his old friend, and he waited.

Before long, there was another knock on the door. Verillio sat up straight, then the door opened and there was Remo Barry standing there, saying, "Verillio, I don't have an eternity."

Verillio was very careful and very precise as he always had been, and he carefully raised the pistol, made sure it was on line, then he squeezed the trigger. He felt only a fractional instant of discomfort as the top of his head blew off and splattered a far wall with flesh and bone and gristle. In the split second before everything stopped, he tried to smile at Remo and he said to himself, "In the name of the Father and. . . ."

The secretary shrieked and fainted. Remo let her drop and walked to the desk. The attaché case was open but it held only money. He felt under the desk

135

and the blades on the shredder basket were still warm. Verillio had left him nothing.

He looked at the money. Stack after stack and $10,000 in each stack. He tried to imagine how many fixes it represented; how many lives destroyed and twisted by the needle that made this money for Verillio; he saw a parade of people passing him by—junkies, children, dying, dead—and he felt no more sympathy for Verillio's dead, skull-shattered body lying there. He stuffed his pockets full of the money. Next, he walked over, gentled the secretary back to consciousness at her desk, and told her she had best call the police. Then he left.

Downstairs, Remo wondered if it were all finished now. Was it all over with Verillio's death? He thought not. There was still a mountain of heroin somewhere and as long as it was out there somewhere, it meant that men would try to sell it. They would fight over it; they would kill for it; and there would be need of Remo Williams, the Destroyer.

Remo walked down the street, thinking, and behind him he heard the wail of sirens headed, no doubt, for Verillio's office. He kept walking and then he was standing in front of a church, a beautiful church. On impulse he went in.

The church was ornate and as beautiful inside. The seats seemed to be hand carved, the altar was magnificent—celebrating the life of Jesus and God. Remo could feel love and worship in the air and he thought it was good for men to have gods to love. He felt in his pocket for the money and it was there, then he saw a young, balding priest standing in the rear of the church and he walked over to him, pulled the money out of his pocket, dropped it onto a small table and said, "For you, Father. To continue God's work."

Remo turned and walked away, and Father F. H. Maguire smiled. He had expected a sign from God.

CHAPTER FOURTEEN

But the stuff was rolling. Into Kansas City came ten pounds and Greasy Russo cut the price to start driving out the competition. There would be plenty more where this came from.

And into Vegas came a few pounds—in the casinos downtown and the whorehouses outside the strip —the word came down: the price is going lower. The independent dealers got the word and began angling to try to get themselves lined up with the man who controlled the sales.

And there were the same stories coming out of St. Louis, Philly, Atlanta and Chicago. The dope was rolling. It was just a trickle now. . .just a few pounds . . .probably brought out in private cars. . .but it was coming.

The trickle would turn into a pour, then into a wave, and when it got split up and scattered around America's major cities, the big fix would be on, America's chance to break the back of the narcotics trade would be lost.

America's allies were angry now, too. France had wanted to handle this and was now pointedly expressing regret that America had blundered. Great Britain and Japan too. What happened in America happened in their countries as well. They wanted the narcotics movers wiped out. If America couldn't do it, well, then, they just might have to fall back on their own resources.

It was noon. Remo had gone back to his New York apartment and called Smith on the scrambler phone.

"Verillio's dead," Remo said.

Smith could not have cared less. "Have you found the heroin?"

"Not yet."

"Not yet? What are you waiting for?"

"I'm waiting for you and all your stupid Dick Tracy snooperscopes to find it"

"Don't be smart. The supplies are getting out. We don't know how and it's just a little bit. But we've got to find the main source of supply."

"Won't Verillio being dead stop it?" Remo asked.

"Use your head. That'll stop it for about five minutes and then somebody else is going to be moving it. What you have to do is find it. And fast. You must act quickly."

"Thanks a lot for the great advice."

"Try following it for a change."

It was a race but Smith hung up first. Score one for him.

Remo looked around the room. On the couch was the pile of equipment he had bought at the sporting goods store on the way over. Chiun had studiously ignored it ever since Remo came in the door. Chiun was still mad because Remo had missed dinner last night after Chiun had made special lobster.

Chiun now sat on the floor watching Myron Brisbane, psychiatrist at large. "Chiun," Remo said,

"You've got to give me a hand with those bodies. The bathroom's getting disgusting, even with the ice."

Chiun stared at the television and mumbled something to Remo. It sounded like "my arteries. . .the strain."

"Come on, Chiun, dammit," Remo said.

"I am too old for that kind of thing."

"You weren't too old to kill them," Remo said.

"Shhhh," Chiun said, holding up a finger for silence and staring at the television.

Remo muttered something about the deceit of Orientals, especially Koreans, and picked up the heavy package and carried it into the bathroom. He did not see Chiun stick out his tongue at Remo's back.

Inside the bathroom, Remo looked at the three bodies crowded into the bathtub, crushed ice packed tightly around them.

Remo dropped his package with a snarl and snapped the heavy twine that wrapped it. From the heavy brown paper, he extracted three duffle bags and three diver's wet suits.

He yanked the top body in the grouping out of the tub onto the tile floor, and began to yank the black foam rubber pants over the dead man's suit clothes. Then he pulled on the long-sleeved black rubber jacket, snapped and zipped both of them shut. He pulled a rubber helmet onto the corpse, then outside rubber booties, and forced the body into one of the duffle bags. He stuffed a towel in on top of the body so no one could look in at the bag's contents and locked it with a padlock.

He repeated the process with the other two bodies in the tub. When he was done the light blue tile floor was sloshy with water and melting ice, but the bodies were packed safely away in the canvas military duffle bags.

Remo stood them up against the sink and walked out again into the living room.

"You going to help me with these? he asked Chiun.

Chiun feigned sleep.

Remo knew when he had lost. "The next time you kill somebody, you get rid of them. I don't even want to know you."

Chiun's eyes were still closed and Remo said out loud, "A sleeping man can't watch television. No point in wasting electricity," and then he walked over and turned off the television.

Remo went back into the bathroom. He hoisted one duffle bag up to his shoulder, catching the body inside at the waist with his shoulder and balancing it there neatly. He grabbed the other duffles by their center handles, one in each hand, straightened up and walked back out into the living room where the television set again was on.

The secret was in motion, and Remo imperceptibly kept the two bags he was holding in his hands swinging gently and the one on his shoulder rocking. He kept them moving all the time, so they never got a chance to become dead weight and he never had a chance to feel their six hundred pounds of weight.

Downstairs the doorman gave him a quizzical look, but hailed a cab. The cabbie stopped and made no offer to help his passenger with his odd luggage, so the passenger tossed it into the back seat himself. ─"Kennedy Airport," he said. The cab driver groused a little because he did not generally make out so well tip-wise on those long hauls, preferring short trips instead. Then on the trip he let his passenger in on his philosophy for the good life, which was that the world would be an all right place if it weren't for the jews, spicks, wops, niggers and polacks, *you ain't jewish or italian, are you, mister?* It was inferior people that made an inferior world, laziness was built into some of those types.

He stopped at Eastern Airlines as he was told and made no effort to help his passenger, who took only one of the bags and told him to wait. He watched through the window. Inside his fare bought a ticket at the counter and checked in the duffle bag of luggage, then the fare came back out and got into the cab. They drove down to the National Airlines ticket office which wasn't far, and did not really give the cab-driver much time to explain about the laziness of most races except his own. There they were already, again his fare lugged out the duffle bag himself and went in, checked the bag after buying a ticket with cash, then he was out in the cab again.

The next stop in line was TWA. The passenger took the third bag, bought a ticket there and checked his duffle bag. The cabbie turned his head for a moment and when he looked around again, his fare was gone. He waited and when the fare didn't return, he got out of the cab. He did not see him on the side-walk and inside he did not see him anywhere in the TWA lounge, and—cursing all jews, guineas and spiks—he went inside and asked the clerk what had happened to the man who checked the duffle bag.

"Oh, you mean, Mister Gonzales," the clerk said, looking at the slip before him. "Well, he had to rush to catch his plane for Puerto Rico. He said that if you came in, I should tell you he'd get you the next time."

But the man known momentarily as Mister Gonzales was not on his way to Puerto Rico. He was sitting in one of the small jump seats on a helicopter headed for Newark Airport.

The duffle bag that belonged to Mr. Gonzales was now being loaded into the rear of the San Juan plane. And another duffle bag just like it, but belonging to Mr. Aronovitz was being loaded into the back of the Anchorage plane. And a third duffle bag, owned by Mr. Botticelli, was already aboard the Chicago plane.

But in Chicago and San Juan and Anchorage, no Mr. Gonzales or Mr. Aronovitz or Mr. Botticelli would call for the bags. They would sit in the terminals for a few days or maybe even a week, then the smell would begin to come through the rubber suits and the police of three cities would have an airport mystery.

That would really stir the pot but he hoped everything would be over before then, thought Remo Williams, now known as Remo Barry—sometimes Mr. Gonzales, Mr. Aronovitz and Mr. Botticelli—as he sat in the helicopter looking down at the meadows, as the chopper lowered for a landing at Newark Airport.

CHAPTER FIFTEEN

The Conwell Funeral Home sat on a tired little side street in Hudson. It was located behind a supermarket, in an old frame building that dated back to the revolutionary war, and in the back yard was a giant oak tree under which George Washington once held a council of war.

The Conwell Funeral Home was very Wasp, very proper, and they simply did not like to bury just any Italian. But Dominic Verillio of course was another story. Why, Mr. Verillio wasn't even really like an Italian or even a Catholic, for that matter.

Why, he was a friend of the mayor's; he belonged to the Museum Society, gave to charities and was active in civic and social work. It was only an accident of birth that gave him an Italian name. The poor man must have suffered so to take his own life because of the pressure of overwork—work for the good of the people, you could count on that—and so funeral services would be held at Conwell's. A call from City Hall had stressed that they must be held immediately, that very day, with the funeral to be held tomorrow.

So there had been a private visitation that afternoon and men in cars, big, black cars and hardfaced men, had come to the funeral home all afternoon.

They had bent a knee at the sealed coffin containing Dominic Verillio's body. They had blessed themselves and left. Not a few of them wondered what had happened to their down payment money for the heroin.

The same men had sent flowers and the flowers had filled not only the small chapel for Dominic Verillio, but the entire first floor of the funeral home. Additional floral pieces were stacked outside on the front porch and still they came from all over the country.

Pietro Scubisci left his bag of peppers inside his car when he came in to bid farewell to Don Dominic. It was not like the old days at all. In the old days, they would have stayed at the funeral home. They would have taken it over. They would have rented entire hotels, so that there would be accommodations for all those who wanted to help send off the spirit of Don Dominic.

But today, Pietro sighed. It was impossible. The feds with their cameras, their microphones and their agents were all over and one could stop only for a moment before having to move on. The world changes. It was probably a good idea to rush the services before the feds could annoy everybody who showed up.

But still it would have been nice to send Don Dominic into the hands of God with a proper ceremony. There was no doubt that he was going to God. Had not Pietro's own daughter said that Don Dominic was going against a god? She must have meant going to God.

Pietro Scubisci bent his knee at the coffin and wiped a tear from his face. Don Dominic Verillio was a widower and no matter what Angela said there had been no children and so no one for Pietro to say goodbye to. Because of her obvious grief, however, he said goodbye to the beautiful young woman standing at the back of the chapel. She had the kind of face that Etruscans dreamed of and the bones looked familiar.

She wept and when Pietro Scubisci patted her on the shoulder, she said, "Grazie, Don Pietro." He looked hard at her but could not remember where he had seen that face. And then he went out into his car, told his driver to get moving to Atlantic City where there would be a conference about leadership and Pietro might have the votes. But who had the heroin?

Scubisci and the other Mafia men had arrived in the afternoon and there were more or less public ceremonies that night. Mayor Hansen was there looking dignified and vacuous, with his daughter, Cynthia, who looked truly grieved, and her mother, a dark woman who only a few persons knew had a drinking problem. She wept uncontrollably. There was Police Chief Brian Dugan because, after all, Verillio was the biggest contributor to the PAL and there was Horgan, the editor, and the Rt. Rev. Msgr. Joseph Antoni. In the back there was Remo Williams, who sat and watched the crowd.

Monsignor Antoni had revised his Columbus Day speech for the occasion. He spoke of Michelangelo and Leonardo DaVinci, of Christopher Columbus and Enrico Fermi. He spoke of Verdi, Caruso, Pope John XXIII and of Frank Sinatra. He said that against this panoply of greatness, of service to mankind, of progress and beauty, Dominic Verillio surely stood, joined with them in strong array against the more sensational exploitations of a handful of over-rated gangsters, belief in whose existence blasphemed against the Italian people. When he said that, he glared angrily at Horgan, who had personally written a long, involved obituary of Verillio, hinting at the mystery in his life and making his opinions clear without ever stating them.

From his seat in the rear of the sweaty little room, Remo watched them all. Mayor Hansen, sitting erect, mixing his small repertoire of facial expressions carefully: one from column *a* for the eyes; another from column *b* for the mouth, alternately looking respectful, thoughtful, grieved, contemplative, and then respectful again.

Remo watched him carefully. It was the first time he had seen him, since Cynthia seemed intent on keeping the two of them apart, and Remo felt the frustration one often feels in dealing with a public man. It takes a lot of digging to get beneath the public face to find out what's really going on and often one finds nothing's going on. The private face is as stupid as the public face.

Still he might have the heroin. Remo would have to find out.

And there was Mrs. Hansen, an Italian looking woman, a woman of real beauty, but obviously now well along the road to alcoholism. She was immaculately groomed, but there were the few telltale signs. The slight disjunctive trembling of the hands, the shifting of weight from one foot to the other, the trapped look deep behind the eyes. She was deep in a personal grief that her husband either did not understand or did not recognize. But she wept to herself continuously. She had lost something with Verillio's death.

Cynthia was there too. She had been there all day, in grief also, and in grief, drawn near to her mother. She did not look at Remo. Perhaps she did not even see him, but he looked at her, felt the stirrings rising in him and wondered what she was doing afterwards.

Horgan was a sphinx, sitting in the front row, next to the police chief, chatting, smiling often; he and Dugan the only two men civilized enough to have fun at a wake.

There were other people that Remo didn't know. He looked at their faces and could not tell anything about their relationship with Verillio. So he leaned over and asked a man next to him, loudly: "He's a suicide, isn't he? How can they bury him in hallowed ground? What's that priest doing here? Isn't suicide a sin? He's going straight to hell, isn't he? What is this all about?"

He watched carefully—saw shock in Mrs. Hansen's face and stupidity in her husband's, saw hate and anger in Cynthia's face, outrage in the face of the police chief and the editor.

Then there was another face that came into the room and the face coughed. It was Willie the Plumber Palumbo. He stood in the back of the room and looked around. Then his eyes met Remo's and Remo smiled, Willie the Plumber turned away and left rapidly before anyone could see the dark splotch on the front of his pants.

Somebody in that room knew about the heroin. But who? Remo had to find out.

Willie the Plumber Palumbo already had found out. And it did not really surprise him. True, he did

148

not yet know where the heroin actually was, but that would be next. And in the meantime he now knew who the boss was and he knew that it was all clear sailing for Willie Palumbo.

He had already carried out his first assignment, letting the Mafiosi in Atlantic City know that the narcotics were still going to be moved, and by tomorrow the Mafiosi around the country would have to deal with him. He would not be the leader of leaders. He did not delude himself. But he would be the man with the key to the heroin and that was just as good. Millions of dollars would be his. Millions. Women. New cars. Anything he wanted.

But first he must make sure that he had a chance to enjoy it all. That meant something must be done about Remo Barry.

Willie the Plumber stopped at an outside telephone booth near the Conwell Funeral Home and dialed a number. He waited while it rang, cursing the uncomfortable dampness of his trousers, and finally after nine rings the phone was answered.

"Hudson Police," the woman's voice said.

"Give me Extension 235," Willie the Plumber said, thankful he was not calling to report a fire. The whole world could have burned down before the phone at headquarters was answered.

Later Remo waited in the parking lot behind the funeral home, standing next to the car he had rented at Newark Airport and kept an eye out for Cynthia Hansen, whose city Chevrolet, black and dented, was still in the lot.

A green Chevrolet bearing three men pulled in through the narrow driveway into the parking lot and pulled up alongside Remo.

The driver rolled down his window and looked at Remo. If he had worn a neon sign that said *cop*, he couldn't have been more obvious.

"Your name Remo?" he said.

Remo nodded.

"I've got a message for you," the driver said. He was husky and graying, his face was set in a perpetual grin.

"Oh," Remo said, "what's the message?" and stepped closer to the car, pretending not to notice the man in the back seat reach for the door handle.

And then Remo had a gun stuck into his face by the driver, the man in the back seat was behind him, expertly frisking him, putting his own gun against the back of Remo's neck. He herded Remo into the backseat and kept the gun on him as the driver peeled off and sped away. Through the window, as the car pulled out of the driveway, Remo could see Mayor Hansen and his wife and his daughter walk slowly down the funeral home stairs, but they did not see him.

"What's the message?" Remo said again to the driver's thick neck.

"You'll get it soon enough," the driver said and chuckled. "Ain't that right? He's gonna get the message."

He turned right on the city's main drag, a few blocks later turned left, and then drove straight on, toward the Hudson River, down into the city's decaying dock area where rotted old barges vied for space with burned out pilings.

They drove out on an old poured-cement pier, against which was tied the metal hulk of a ship which

150

had been gutted by a fire months before and was now waiting for the start of salvage work.

The pier was dark and empty and, except for the scurrying of a few rats, they were alone.

The policeman in the back with Remo poked him in the ribs with the gun. "Get out, wise guy."

Remo allowed himself to be herded up a wooden gangplank onto the ship at gunpoint, then into the wheelhouse on the main deck where the cop behind him pushed him hard against the opposite wall.

Remo turned and faced the three policemen. "What's this all about, fellas?" he asked.

"You been causing a lot of trouble," the one who had been driving said.

"I'm just a reporter. Trying to get a story," Remo protested.

"Save that crap for somebody who believes it," the driver said. "We want to know who sent you. A simple question. All it takes is a simple answer."

"I keep trying to tell people. The *Intelligentsia Annual*. I write for them."

"What are you, their narcotics expert? That's a funny thing for that kind of a magazine."

"It's just my assignment. I do what I'm told."

"So do we," the driver said, "so I want you to know it's nothing personal."

He opened a cabinet inside the room and took out a blowtorch. He pumped it a few times and then lit it with a cigarette lighter. The flame hissed out—blue, weak—he put it on the floor. "All right, boys," he said, "get him."

He drew his own pistol and the other two policemen put theirs away. Then they advanced on Remo who backed up as far in the small room as he could.

151

They each grabbed one of his arms and they smirked as he struggled to pull himself free. Fat chance, they thought, but he was tenacious and he skittered along the floor a little bit and then they were closer to the man with the gun than they ought to be, but nothing serious, they had him.

Then they didn't have him, and they each felt a sharp crack on the temple and the driver who had held his gun on the three of them found the gun ripped from his hand and tossed through a burned out window opening. Seconds later, it hit water far below with a splash and then Remo had the blowtorch and he was raising the flame.

The other two detectives behind Remo were unconscious or dead. But they were down and still and now Remo blocked the way to the door.

The blowtorch flame hissed louder, yellower as Remo turned it up, then he said, "All right, officer, now we're going to talk."

The policeman looked anxiously around the room. There was no way out. And his men on the floor had not stirred. They might be dead. Could he get to one of them to get a gun?

Remo moved over toward the two men.

"We'll start out easy," Remo said. "What do you know about Ocean Wheel trucks?"

"Nothing," the policeman said. He started to say "I never heard of them" but never got the words out because his mouth was occupied with screaming as a blowtorch flame seared the back of his hand.

"Try again," Remo said. "That answer was not responsive."

The policeman was shaken. "I saw some once," he stammered. "Coming off the pier. Only time I ever

152

saw them. But they vanished. Someplace on the way out of town. We looked for them, but nobody knows where they went."

Remo turned the flame up higher. "Okay, who do you take orders from?"

"Used to be Gasso."

"Gasso's dead," Remo said.

"I know. Now it's Willie the Plumber. He called us tonight. Told us to get you."

"Who's his boss?"

"Verillio."

"Verillo's dead," Remo said. "Who's Willie the Plumber's new boss?"

"I don't know," the cop said and flinched as the flame came closer to his good hand. "Somebody in City Hall. It's always been somebody in City Hall."

"Not the chief? Not Dugan?"

"No, he's honest. All he's got is numbers and whores," the policeman said, and Remo knew he was telling the truth.

"How about the mayor? Hansen?"

"I don't know," the policeman said. "I don't know." And again Remo knew he was telling the truth.

"Listen," the policeman said, "give me a break. Let me work with you. I'll find out who's running things. I can help you. You can use a guy with brains. Look how good I set up those narco people. They trusted my badge and I unsprung their trap. They were easy kills. I can help you the same way."

He looked at Remo's face hopefully, but Remo was impassive and the policeman knew his offer was going to be turned down, so he did the only thing left to him. He dove for the bodies of the two policemen

153

on the floor, trying to pull a gun from under one of their jackets. His hand circled the butt of one of the guns and then his hand didn't work anymore. He looked up just in time to see a hand speed down toward his up-looking face and he felt nothing after the facial bones splintered.

Remo looked at the three dead men on the wooden floor of the wheelhouse and for a moment felt disgusted with himself. Then his mind went back to the cruise ship and the picture of the young junkie, racked by drugs and fever, and he looked down at the three dead cops who had done their part to protect that kind of traffic. Then he felt a rage turn his body hot, and he did the kind of thing Remo Williams never did. He advertised.

Poor Skorich, at least, had died in the line of duty. Departmental honors. Something for his family to cling to. But these three swine . . . Remo would do his best to make sure there were no brass bands or grieving city for their deaths.

When the sun came up the next morning, the black hulk of the ship would be outlined, silhouetted black against the sun's early rays. As the sun rose higher, the ship would begin to take form, and the early men on the docks would look at it as they always did, without real interest because it didn't mean a day's pay. But sometime during the morning, some of them would look again and they would look at the anchor and then they would look again and some of them would cross themselves, because hanging from the anchor's points, the dull points driven through their bodies, twisted like some terrible fish, would be the three policemen, hooked and hung out to dry. And very dead.

154

CHAPTER SIXTEEN

Myron Horowitz was in love. Not only was his girl the most beautiful girl in the world, but she was going to make him rich—rich in a way that no one on Pelham Parkway could understand.

Had she not built for him this new drug plant? Probably unique in the world. Fully-automated. It needed only one person to operate it and he was that one person, Myron Horowitz, Rutgers University, 1968, R.P. Just him and no one else, except of course the janitor whom he had sent home tonight, and a billing service that he used to handle his paperwork.

He supposed it was business that made her ask him to meet her tonight at the factory. He supposed it was, but he was ready in case it wasn't, and so he checked the sofa in his office. It was neat and clean and the stereo was playing softly; he had out a bottle of Chivas Regal and two glasses, was ready in case there was a chance to talk about anything but business.

Late night meetings were not unusual, not when you considered that in a secret basement below the one-story building were hidden four tractor trailers, their drivers frozen to death, but their cargos still intact, ready to make up into powders and pills and ointments and syrups. Any strength.

Four trailer loads. Fifty tons of 98 per cent pure heroin. Fifty tons. And the U.S. drug peddlers used maybe eight tons a year. Six years' supply. Fifty tons. Horowitz was sitting on it.

Fifty tons. Horowitz often did the arithmetic. Fifty tons was 100,000 pounds and when it was cut and cut and cut and thinned at each step along the line, a pound would have a street value of over $100,000. For each pound. And he was sitting on 100,000 pounds.

He knew there had been problems with delivery. Everything was being watched carefully. But he had gotten some out in aspirin bottles and some as stomach powders and all in all he had probably gotten out maybe 100 pounds in the last two weeks. That was $10 million worth when it got down to the users.

Myron Horowitz never considered the morality of what he was doing. Narcotics were like alcohol. A little bit never hurt anybody. Didn't everyone know that most doctors use narcotics regularly? And they still practiced medicine and performed operations and delivered babies and nobody seemed to get upset about it. In a way, maybe he was even doing a service. By making more of it available in a better grade, maybe he was helping to stop accidental deaths from contaminated drugs and if users did not have to steal drugs maybe he could reduce the crime rate a little.

Headlights flashed out in front of his factory and he picked up the telephone and dialed the number of the Parrish Electronic Protective Service. "This is Myron Horowitz, Code 36-43-71. I'm opening the

156

front door at Liberty Drugs on Liberty Road. Okay. Right."

He hung up the phone and walked to the front door. Through the frosted glass, he could see the outline of the familiar dark sedan as it pulled around behind the building, out of sight of the road. He waited a moment, then heard footsteps and opened the door.

Cynthia Hansen stepped inside quickly and he closed the door behind her.

He turned and followed her down the dark hallway to his office ahead, where two large lamps burned. As he followed her he could not resist reaching out and cupping her cheeks in his hands but she stopped short and said chillingly, "This is business, Myron."

He removed his hands reluctantly. "Lately, it's always business," he whined.

"A lot of things have happened," she said. "I just haven't been in the mood. Things will be back to normal soon," she said and gave him just the hint of a smile.

It was enough to bolster Myron Horowitz's spirits —to raise his hopes that the stereo, the Chivas Regal and the open couch might yet have an effect.

Cynthia Hansen walked into the office and turned off the stereo. She put the bottle of Chivas Regal back into the portable bar and put the glasses away. Then she took a chair and sat before the desk, facing Horowitz who sat behind the desk.

She wasted no time. "The shipment downstairs. How much can you package?"

"The plant's working real well now," he said. "I can turn out 500 pounds of heroin in different forms in a week. But can you move it? That's been the problem, hasn't it?"

"Yes," she said, "that's been the problem. And the government has had some snooper in and he's been causing trouble."

"I read about Verillio. He must have really been under pressure to blow his own brains out. I thought these thugs never did that."

"Mister Verillio to you," Cynthia Hansen said. "And don't ever think he was a thug. He died so that there'd be no link to me and to you. Don't forget it."

"I'm sorry, Cynthia," Horowitz stammered. "I didn't mean. . . ."

"Forget it," she said. "Anyway this federal man, this Remo Barry. He should be out of it by now. Some of the boys took care of him tonight. And I've found out how to make deliveries. You sure you can do 500 pounds a week?"

"At least 500 pounds," he said. "And 98 per cent pure heroin. Do you know what that's worth?" he asked.

"Better than you do," she said. "Fifty million on the street. But we're wholesalers. To us, only one-fifth of that. Ten million."

"But every week," Horowitz said. "Ten million every week. And we can go on forever."

"Just don't get careless. I've gone to a lot of trouble to set this up." She lit a cigarette. "I've let the leaders know that the stuff is still available, same prices, same quality, same terms. And now I can guarantee delivery."

"How are we going to do that? Everything's being watched."

"We're going to ship it out with carrots."

"Carrots?"

"Yes, carrots. In vegetable trucks. Don't worry

about it, it'll work. And I want to move this stuff out of here as fast as I can, then I want to burn this place down, cover it over with dirt, and go live someplace civilized."

"The two of us," Horowitz said.

"Hmm? Yes, the two of us, Myron," she said. "Keep preparing the stuff and stashing it. I'll be in touch with you about delivery." She stubbed out her cigarette and stood up.

"Cynthia?"

"What?"

"How about tonight?" he said. "Please."

"I've told you. I'm not in the mood."

"I bet you're in the mood when you're with that hairy ape I've seen you with."

"No. He's got nothing to do with it," she said. "Besides he's dead." And she thought of Remo who by now was also dead and she smiled at Myron and said, "I'm sorry, Myron. I'm really just not in the mood."

She left quickly. Myron watched her go out the door, then phoned the protective service again to let them know he had opened the door. While he was on the phone he opened the center drawer of his desk, took out a small bottle labelled aspirins and popped one of the pills into his mouth. It was good for the nerves, even better than real aspirin.

159

CHAPTER SEVENTEEN

The first word came from Great Britain. It came unofficially, so that it could be denied if need be, but it came accurately.

Her Majesty's Government regarded the lack of effective action on the part of the United States regarding the massive heroin shipment as inexcusable error. And since so much of Great Britain's narcotics traffic was tied hand-to-hand with the availability of drugs in the United States, Her Majesty's Government had decided it must protect its own best interests.

And in Charing Mews, a hard-faced man who looked like Hoagy Carmichael put his exploding briefcase in the back seat of his supercharged Bentley to begin the drive to London Airport for a BOAC plane to New York.

Elysee Palace shared Her Majesty's Government's feelings exactly. After all, had not France offered to close down the heroin operation and had not the White House prevented them from doing so? And did not the American ineptitude now threaten continued friendly relations and cooperation in the field of law enforcement between the two countries?

Therefore, the government of France would now feel free to take whatever steps were necessary to close down this narcotics operation and in the process protect France's international reputation as a battler against the drug menace.

And Japan, too, had heard. It joined in the general panic at the prospect of so many tons of heroin being moved openly into the world's illegal narcotics market. And from Tokyo also came the same message, unofficially of course: "whatever steps we feel are necessary."

In his office at Folcroft Sanatorium, Dr. Harold W. Smith, head of CURE, read the reports.

They meant manpower. It meant that these governments would send in to the United States their top operatives, gun-happy lunatics to try to track down the heroin gang. What the hell did they think they could do that Remo Williams couldn't do? Except get in Remo's way.

Smith looked at the reports again. He could tell the President that he was pulling Williams off the assignment. He would be justified in doing that.

Then Smith pursed his lips and thought of the pictures and reports he had shown to Remo: the stories of agony those dry statistics told; the young children hooked on drugs; the addict infants born to junkie mothers; the lives ruined and lost; the millions stolen and wasted. He thought of his daughter now cold-turkeying it at a farm in Vermont, and he pulled back his hand which had strayed close to the special White House telephone.

America's best hope to crack the case was Remo Williams, the Destroyer.

In the hope of preserving international relations, Smith prayed softly that none of the friendly countries' operatives would get in Remo's way.

CHAPTER EIGHTEEN

Don Dominic Verillio had been laid to his eternal rest in the green rolling hills of a cemetery fifteen miles outside the city, where the air was still semi-breathable and where birds sang.

A police motorcycle escort and honor guard had led the hearse and the flower car. One hundred persons had followed in limousines and stood at the graveside, in early morning dew, as the final funeral rites were held.

Then people had separated and gone their own ways.

Willie the Plumber Palumbo had been directed to take Mrs. Hansen, the mayor's wife, back to her home. She was still crying uncontrollably.

Cynthia Hansen joined Mayor Hansen in driving back to City Hall. She left him at the door of his office and went to her own office.

Craig Hansen took off his homburg, which he disliked wearing because he felt it added too much age to his face, and stepped through the massive wooden door into his office.

A man sat there, in his chair, feet up on his desk, reading the sports section of the *Daily News*.

The man put down the paper and looked up as the

mayor walked in. "Hello, Hansen," he said. "I've been waiting for you."

Hansen had seen the man last night at the funeral home. It was that writer fellow, Remo something or other, who had been pestering Cynthia. Well, Mayor Craig Hansen would make short work of him.

"Hi there, fellow," he said, tossing his homburg onto the fourteen-foot long mahogany table. "Something I can do for you?"

Remo stood up. "Yeah, Hansen. Where's the heroin?"

"It's a terrible problem, the entire problem of drug addiction," Hansen said. "It feeds at the vitals of America and there is no real cure for any of our urban ills until this social cancer is removed from the body politic."

Hansen had walked over by his desk and Remo stepped aside to make room for Hansen in the mayor's chair.

"Yeah, but where is it?" Remo persisted.

"Where is it at? That's the question we continuously hear in the streets of the city. I regard it as an anguished cry for help from those upon whose strength and vigor the city relies for its renewed vitality," Hansen said. "Can there be any doubt. . . ."

As he talked, Remo looked at the vapid, bland face and he knew that Mayor Craig Hansen could no more plot a heroin operation than he could clean a street. He looked closely at his face, all of it seemingly in correct proportions—the right shape—but apparently without a bone in it.

And Remo thought of other faces. Hansen's wife, with her fine Roman lines. And Verillio who, before his own bullet had removed the top of his skull, had worn a face with character and strength. And he thought of Cynthia Hansen and he realized suddenly where that fine Etruscan face had come from, and why Mrs. Hansen had cried so much, and why Verillio had conceded his own death so quickly.

Mayor Hansen had spun toward the window and was staring through the dirty dusty glass at the city —his city—and his voice droned on, "without social strength, no real progress is possible, particularly inasmuch as our real estate tax base. . . ." and he continued on as Remo slipped outside and quietly closed the door behind him.

Remo walked past a startled clerk-typist and toward the door to Cynthia's office. He stepped inside silently and locked the door behind him.

Cynthia was seated at her desk, her head down, still crying, her body racked with sobs.

She wore a black dress that celebrated her body. As Remo stood there and watched her, slowly she realized someone's presence. She looked up and saw him. Shock slowly blasted sorrow from her face.

"You. . . ." she said.

"Me. Your goons last night missed."

And Cynthia, whose tears were for Remo as well as Verillio, turned shock into anger and fear into hatred, snarling, "You bastard."

She stood up and reached for her top right hand desk drawer. Remo knew it would be a gun. But he had no eyes for a gun, only for her breasts and her long waist, and he was on her, rolling her around, away from the open drawer, around the front of the desk. Then his weight was on her. He had her dress up around her hips, she was pinned and Remo was in her.

164

"Just one for the road, baby," he said.

She hissed at him, "I hate you, you bastard, I hate you."

Remo stayed working at her, pressing into her at her desk. The touch and the contact worked slowly and her fury again turned back to tears, as she said, "How could you? He was my father."

Remo said, "I didn't know."

"You didn't really think that creep inside could sire me, did you?" Cynthia asked. It didn't really seem to call for an answer so instead Remo just kept stroking away at Cynthia Hansen, the daughter of Don Dominic Verillio.

Willie the Plumber Palumbo had coughed savagely several times and paused, leaning on the door of his blue Eldorado, until his eyes cleared and his breath came back. Then he closed the door, not slamming it too hard, and walked around to open the door for Mrs. Hansen.

Even now, now that he knew she had been Verillio's mistress for years, he still felt her tears were excessive. But that was all right in Willie's book. Let her practice, he thought grimly. She'll soon be crying all over again at the loss of a daughter.

He helped Mrs. Hansen up the stairs of her home and turned her over to the mercies of the family maid. Then he went back to his car and began the leisurely drive downtown to City Hall.

Willie had been promoted yesterday and it had been his third shock of the day. First, there had been Gasso. And then Verillio. And then the ultimate shock of Cynthia Hansen telling him that she alone controlled the heroin and that she needed him now to be her number one man.

He had always known that Verillio had had a boss, and probably one in City Hall, but he had always thought it was the mayor, not the daughter. And now that he thought about it, about her tears and her honest mourning, he wouldn't be surprised if there were more to it than just the fact that she was Verillio's partner and the one with the heroin. There had to be something more to it than that.

She was quick, though. He had to admit it. She had done the right things. She had told him to contact the leaders in Atlantic City to tell them the deal was still on. She had told him to get the narcotics cops to finish off Remo Barry. And she had seemed excited when he had told her about the funny machine that tracked down carrots and turnips and poppies. She had even kissed him on the cheek.

No matter. No matter. She was not Sicilian and she was a woman. She was going to remain Willie the Plumber's boss just long enough to lead him to the heroin and then she was going to join her friend, Mr. Verillio, in a very cold grave. In Willie's city, there would be room for only one boss—and he would be it.

But for the time being, he'd have to play it cute, Willie the Plumber told himself as he parked his Eldorado in the lot behind City Hall in a spot reserved for the City Clerk.

He was preparing his opening pleasantry as he rode up in the elevator, and he almost had the words out of his mouth as he used the symbol of his new status, the key Cynthia had given him to her City

166

Hall office. He never got the words out because there she was, dress hiked up around her ass, being humped in front of her desk by that bastard again, that Remo Barry, who Willie thought had been taken care of last night by the narcos.

Willie the Plumber did not believe in using a bean shooter when a howitzer would do. And he did not understand all the niceties of Gasso, Verillio and probably the narco cops. What is more, he didn't care. So he reached into his jacket and pulled out his pistol. Then the man known as Remo turned around and looked into Willie the Plumber's eyes. Remo's eyes were cold and deadly, like brown ice, and Willie the Plumber knew what Gasso and Verillio must have felt just before they died.

Remo moved. Willie's finger froze on the trigger and Remo was at him. Then Remo was throwing his floater stroke which if it had hit could have cut Willie in half.

Bu tunconsciously, Willie the Plumber had discovered one of the great secrets of Oriental combat: the fastest way out of a path is to collapse. Willie collapsed, fainted dead on the floor, and Remo's floater stroke, without a target to use up its energy, continued forward—missing Willie—and all its force, instead of destroying some target, raced back along his own arm. The force was just too much for muscle to take and Remo's shoulder dislocated from its socket. The sudden wrench of pain knocked him out and put him unconscious on the floor next to the twisted body of Willie the Plumber who lay there, terrified and coughing even in his sleep.

CHAPTER NINETEEN

Remo shivered.

He felt cold and he forced his mind to quicken his body rhythms and his blood began flowing faster, carrying warmth throughout his body. It was only when he was warm that he realized his shoulder hurt.

He opened his eyes slowly. He was on the stone floor of some kind of factory or warehouse building and it was not just cold in his imagination. He could see swirls of cold air vapor moving slowly across the floor and when he pushed himself into a sitting position he discovered his left arm was useless.

Chiun had made him a superman, but Chiun could do nothing about changing the human anatomy. Shoulder joints were not designed to withstand the force Remo had applied to his own, no more than knees were designed to resist the tearing and pulling put on them by two-hundred-eighty-pound giants who could run the hundred in 9.5 in football garb. Maybe in twenty generations of evolution. But not yet.

And it was cold. Cynthia Hansen shivered as she stood in front of him, leaning against a trailer truck. Remo shook his eyes into focus. The truck said Chelsea Trucking but there were four of them in a row, parked neatly, and Remo knew he had found the four Ocean Wheel trucks that had carried the heroin.

But more important than the four trailers and the cold was something else, this pistol Cynthia Hansen held in her hand, pointed at Remo's head.

Remo struggled to his feet and swayed groggily back and forth. His arm was really shot. He could tell. There was no sense of belonging, no sense of muscle, just a numbing pain somewhere south of his left shoulder.

"Where are we?" he asked, speaking more thickly than was necessary.

"You're in the place you've been looking for. Our drug factory. These are the trucks of heroin," Cynthia said.

Remo allowed himself to be impressed. "Enough here for a tidy little nest egg," he said.

"More than enough," she said and he could sense her grasping for the little straw he had held out.

"How'd you get me here?"

"I drove you here. My druggist carried you down from upstairs."

"You've got a partner?" Remo questioned, trying to sound hurt.

Cynthia looked up and saw the door leading to the top of the stairs was tightly shut. "Him? He's an employe," she said.

"There's too much here for one person to spend," Remo said.

"Better one than none," she said, and she shuddered as the cold went through her.

Remo swung his good right arm as if to warm himself and as her eyes went toward the movement, he slid forward a step, imperceptibly, toward her.

"Yeah," he said, "but better two than one."

"It could have been, Remo," she said sadly. "It really could have been."

For the first time she met his eyes full and Remo turned on the warmth in them. He forced his mind to conjure up visions of their sex, under tables, among salami skins, against desks and in chairs. His eyes mirrored exactly what was on his mind and she responded to his eyes.

She said again, "It really could have been. Just you and me."

"Yeah, just the three of us. You, me and your gun," Remo said, swinging his arm again, moving another step closer. "You know," he said, "we've got something. It never took any gun for me to perform."

"It was never like that for me before, either," she said. "But never again. How could I trust you?" she asked, hoping that he could convince her.

"How do women ever trust men? Most of them don't need guns," Remo said.

"I didn't think I needed one," Cynthia said.

Remo answered, "Everything you ever needed you were born with."

Her gun hand wavered slightly. Remo saw it and said, "It would just be you and me." Slowly the gun came down and she was defenseless before him. He was only a few feet away and, dammit, all he could see was that finely chiseled face and that great bosom and long sloping waist, she leaned her face forward and Remo was on her lips with a groan. When she searched his mouth, he heard the gun drop to the floor with a clank.

Then he was moving her, their mouths still joined, but slowly, step by step, he was moving her toward

170

the cab of the first truck. He leaned her against the cab and took his good hand from her breasts and reached up and caught the door handle and opened the door. Then he lifted her up and slid her into the seat. And he had her dress up around her eyes and he forced her legs apart so one was up on the dashboard and he forced himself between her legs, ignoring the pain in his torn shoulder and he put himself in.

The cold was chilling and the cab was uncomfortable, but for Remo, with this woman, it was like an overstuffed bed.

He leaned against her ear and told her, "I always wanted to do it in a truck," and he brought her up to his rhythm.

He kept her there as he kept moving. Her arms came around his head and pulled him close to her face, as she whispered in his ear, "Remo, I love you. I love you. Please. Please."

They were both nearing the end. She was bucking and writhing under him on the seat of the truck and she bit into his ear as they came. He pulled back slightly, not to escape her teeth, but to give himself room to pull her skirt up over her face, so she would not see the blow coming as his good hand came up over his head and then down into her waiting face. Remo felt the bones crunch under his hand and he knew she was dead.

He knew that if he had looked into her face, he might not have been able to do it, and he had to do it. He had to do it in the name of all those teenage junkies who infested the country, whose curse was the source of Cynthia Hansen's riches, and whose lifelong agonies would pay for her pleasures.

Out of hatred, he killed her. But because, in a way, he loved her, he had let her die quickly.

Then Remo pulled away from her and he saw for the first time why the truck cab had seemed crowded. Huddled on the floor in the corner under the steering wheel were the bodies of two men, crowded together for warmth, frozen solid. Remo stared at them unseeing for a moment.

Then in a flame of anger, he brought his hand up again and down hard into the already crushed face beneath the black skirt, this time with hatred only, and said, "That's the biz, sweetheart."

Remo stepped down from the truck cab. He thought to himself sadly that he had left a great deal of himself in the cab along with the twisted body of Cynthia Hansen.

Then he tried to remember her face and found out he could not. Perhaps such memories were only for men. And he was not just a man. He was the Destroyer.

Suddenly he felt cold again.

CHAPTER TWENTY

Myron Horowitz had been humming.

He had helped Cynthia carry that impossible bastard, Remo something or other, down into the deep freeze, had left her down there to shoot him.

He was needed up here. The machines were busy and the pills were spinning out, dropping into bottles labelled "aspirin" but containing a better medicine than all the acetaminphen in the world. Ninety-eight per cent pure heroin. He had taken a tablet that morning before Cynthia arrived and he felt good. Of course, that was no real drug problem because he could stop any time, and he must admit, it did make him feel even more the fine upstanding man that he knew he was. Doctors did it, didn't they? And if he had wanted to, he could have been a doctor.

He was busy monitoring the pill-making machines and he had been humming tunelessly, the kind of humming that a man who will soon be a multi-millionaire can indulge himself in. He did not notice the footsteps behind him.

Finally, when someone cleared his throat and Horowitz turned, he was only mildly surprised that it was not Cynthia Hansen, and not much more surprised that three men stood there. They were funny looking men. If Myron Horowitz had not been a gentleman, he might have giggled. He giggled anyway.

There was this round little man with a head like an egg and a twisty little mustache who said "allo," who must have been a Frenchman because he was carrying an umbrella. There was a silly looking Oriental with thick eyeglasses who just stood there smiling insanely at Myron Horowitz. And there was a very funny one indeed, an enormously fat man who looked like Hoagy Carmichael after six months of forced feeding; he stood there, grinning out of the side of his mouth and clutching the handle of his briefcase with both hands.

Well, Myron Horowitz tried to be polite, and he knew that he would have acted the same, even if he had not had a pill, but it was his time of the day to relax a little and to feel good, so he grinned and said, "Hi, boys. Have a pill?"

He never did know what he said that was wrong because he didn't have a chance to ask before the Oriental pulled out a pistol and put a bullet in his head, as he said to his two companions, "Is preasing you?"

The shot was the first sound Remo Williams heard as he came through the door that, from the inside, did not look like a door and into the room where the pills were made by automated machines. Even now, with Horowitz dead, the machines kept pumping out their deadly medicine in hard little tablets with a steady *tapocketa pocketa*.

Remo Williams was unseen by the three men and he walked up quietly behind the Oriental and snatched the gun from his hand.

Remo skidded the gun across the floor of the drug

factory and the three men wheeled and Remo demanded, "Who the hell are you? The Marx Brothers?"

The man who looked like Hoagy Carmichael answered. In a clipped British accent, he said, "Official business, old man. Just stay out of the way. We're licensed to kill."

"Not around here, you're not, you silly shit," Remo said.

The Englishman lifted his brief case up onto the counter knocking bottles of pills to the floor to make room for it. He began to fumble at the latches.

The Oriental, mistaking Remo's anger for anger, grabbed Remo's bad arm and pivoted under his bad shoulder. He bent forward in the classic ju-jitsu move to throw Remo over his back. Everything was done just right, except he had never done it before to a man whose shoulder was dislocated. All it did to Remo was hurt him, so Remo took his right fist and curled it up into the karate hand mace, bringing it down on top of the Oriental's head with a fearsome crunch.

The Oriental dropped like a wet sock.

"Just a minute, old chap," the Englishman said. "Just let me get this case open," he said, as he fumbled again with the latches.

The little man with the head like an egg and the pointed mustache clutched his umbrella to his side, then pulled his right hand away, peeling out an evil looking foil almost three feet long. He ducked into a fencing pose, shouted *en garde* and lunged forward with the point of the epeé at Remo's stomach. Remo side-stepped and the sword slid harmlessly by his waist.

"Keep him occupied, Hercule," the Englishman called. "I'll be right with you. I've almost got it."

Hercule pulled back his sword and prepared for another lunge. He thrust forward and this time Remo let the blade slip by him, then yanked it out of the Frenchman's hand. Holding it by its uncutting dulled edge, he thumped the Frenchman on the head with the umbrella handle and the Frenchman went into a deep swoon.

Remo dropped the sword and turned to the Englishman. He saw Remo staring at him, and tilted his head to the side slightly so he could smile sardonically at him. "Must say you Yanks are always in such a bloody hurry. Now just hold still a moment, while I get this open. *M* will hear about this defective equipment."

As Remo watched, he fumbled with the latches and then cried out in triumph, "That's it. I've got it now, I've got it," and he pulled up on the handle and it separated from the briefcase.

He aimed the twin points of the handle at Remo's chest, tilted his head and again smiled sardonically. I've had experience with your sort before. The Speckled Polka Dot Gang, don't you know. And let me tell you, you Mafia types can't hold a candle to some of the people I've run into. Well, old boy. Are you ready? Anything you'd like to say? I'll give you a couple of lines in my report. Any last words?"

"Yeah," Remo said. "Up yours, you dizzy bastard." He turned his back and walked away toward the telephone he saw on the desk in the office. The smiling Englishman took careful aim with the attaché case handle, pressed down on the second-bolt-in-from-the-end and shot himself in the foot.

Remo ignored the noise behind him and went inside to call Dr. Harold W. Smith.

CHAPTER TWENTY ONE

Dr. Harold W. Smith knew what to do. The Treasury Department was called immediately and within minutes men in snap-brimmed hats began arriving at the drug factory.

Remo had gone. Inside they found a dead Horowitz, an unconscious Oriental and an unconscious Frenchman. A bloated Englishman, bleeding slightly from a wound in the foot, sat on Horowitz's desk drinking from a bottle of Chivas Regal when they entered. He was on the telephone and he covered the mouthpiece when they came in the door and called out: "Hello, boys. Glad you could join the party. You'll find everything you need. Just handle the paperwork and things'll go a lot smoother."

Then he was back talking into the telephone. "Cedric? That you? You-know-who here. Yes. Biggest one yet. Can we make the next edition? Okay. Grab your pencil and your socks. Here we go. The biggest drug ring in the history of international smuggling was broken up today and the real story is the unsung role played in the case by. . .heh, heh, you know who, on Her Majesty's Secret Service."

At the same time, Dr. Harold W. Smith was on the telephone with the White House. The President sat in his bedroom, his shoes off, listening to the parched voice.

"That matter has been cleared up, Mr. President."

"Thank you," the President said. "And that person?"

"I believe he is well. I will convey your concern."

"And our gratitude."

"And your gratitude," Dr. Smith said before placing his phone back on its red base.

It was noon when the first bulletin came out of Washington across the United Press International ticker. James Horgan, editor of the *Hudson Tribune*, heard the clanking of the bells on the teletype machine and stuck his head out of his office.

His staff studiously ignored the ringing of the bells which generally signalled a major news item. Horgan swore softly and walked to the back of the room where he leaned over the teletype machine, then ripped the yellow sheet of paper from the machine.

He read: ". . . Enough heroin to fuel America's underworld narcotics trade for six years was seized today in a daring daylight raid in Hudson, New Jersey, United States Treasury officials announced."

more to come.   EGF1202WDC

Horgan glanced at the copy, then at the clock. It was 12:03. Three minutes after all the copy should have been gone from the editorial room and out into the composing room on its way into the pages.

He walked back to the city desk where the city editor was trying to do the word game. Can you get twenty-one words in fifteen minutes from effluvium. Average mark, seventeen words. Time limit, twenty minutes.

Horgan tossed the yellow bulletin on the desk in

front of the city editor. "In case you were wondering," he said, "all those bells ringing were not a fire alarm. So there's nothing to worry about. Do you think you might finish that puzzle in time to try to get some news in today's paper?"

The city editor looked at the bulletin, then up at Horgan. "What should I do?" he asked.

Horgan thought for a moment, then picked up the bulletin. "Hold Page One. Then go back to your frigging puzzle and stay out of the way."

Horgan vanished into his office carrying the scrap of paper from the UPI machine. A few moments later, he bellowed "copy" and a copyboy ran in and carried a sheet of white paper out to the city editor.

"Mr. Horgan says start working on this." The copyboy ran to the back of the room to take the latest bulletin off the UPI machine.

Every few minutes, he brought a new bulletin into Horgan's office and seconds later white sheets came out, carefully blending UPI's dry factual reports with the stories of the dead narcotics policemen, the mysterious Remo Barry who had been in town, Verillio's death and the political protection that had been given the narcotics gang.

At 12:17, he stepped out of his office carrying the last sheet of paper.

"How's it read?" he asked his city editor.

"Okay," the editor said. "But do you think we ought to speculate like that?"

"Only until you get somebody around here who can find out a fact." He started to walk away when the city editor called: "You want a byline on this?"

Horgan stopped. "It's going to be one of those Italian mob things again and I just don't need any more

179

flak about being anti-Italian. Put some Italian by-line on it."

The city editor thought for a moment and his eyes strayed to the reference shelf behind the city desk. *History of Great Operas,* he read on the back of one book.

He bent over a sheet of paper and pencilled:
"Set 14 point.
By Joseph Verdi"

CHAPTER TWENTY TWO

When Willie the Plumber Palumbo came to, on the floor of Cynthia Hansen's office, the bitch was gone and so was Remo Barry.

Willie lay there on the heavy carpeting for a few moments, afraid to move for fear the broken bones would hurt. He had seen Gasso's body. He knew what his must look like.

Slowly, exploratorily, he moved his left index finger. He felt no pain. He moved the entire hand. No pain. Then he moved his other hand. And then his feet. At least he was not crippled. When he sat up, he found that he was not hurt at all.

Willie the Plumber scrambled to his feet and paid for the sudden exertion with a violent coughing fit that caused his eyes to blank for a moment.

Then he was all right again. He walked out into the red tiled hall where his cleated heels chipped wax and he walked forward on the balls of his feet to make no noise, heading down the back stairs to the parking lot where his blue Eldorado sat.

He did not know how long he had been out. But any long was too long. Remo Barry must have gotten the girl. He would probably be back for Willie the

Plumber. Well, Willie the Plumber would be long gone.

Willie the Plumber was not simple. Big score or no big score, heroin or no heroin, it was more important to stay alive.

Willie had enough to stay alive for a long time. In an ashcan in his cellar was hidden several hundred thousand dollars in cash and it would be enough to move Willie far across the country, maybe even out of the country, and set him up in a new life.

Willie jumped into his car and sped the few blocks to the old four-family tenement that he had made into a one-family home for himself.

He parked the Cadillac at the curb and took the front stairs two at a time, coughing all the way.

It took him only a few minutes to find a brief case and to empty the money from the ashcan into it. It was $227,000. Willie counted it often.

He closed the brief case and walked out the front door, locking it behind him. He would send the key to his sister-in-law. She could come in and clean it until he sold it.

As he was about to get into his Eldorado, he noticed a smudge on the hood and he walked up to the smudge. He leaned over the shiny hood and exhaled onto the smudge, then put his face down close to the finish as he polished off the smudge with the sleeve of his jacket.

He caught a flash of movement on the other side of the car and tilted his head slightly to catch the reflection in the highly-waxed hood.

A man stood there.

Willie stood up and looked across the car into the deep brown eyes of Remo Williams.

Remo smiled at him, then holding his left arm stiffly at his side, bent down below the level of the car for a moment and picked up something from the gutter.

He stood up, holding a rusty old nail in his right hand. Still smiling at Willie the Plumber, he pressed the tip of the nail into the blue enamelled finish of the hood and pressed. First a tiny piece of paint chipped, and then Remo dragged the nail through the finish, running a scar down the hood of the Eldorado from windshield to grill.

Willie the Plumber looked at the vandalized hood of the shiny car and started to cry. Real tears.

The man named Remo said, "Willie, get in the car." Willie, still crying, slid in behind the wheel. Remo got in the passenger's side.

"Just drive around, Willie," he said.

Willie the Plumber, now sobbing only slightly, drove through the heart of the city and finally picked up an old inadequate highway that passed through the meadows bordering the city's western side.

"Turn here," Remo ordered and Willie the Plumber pulled off the highway into a narrow two-lane blacktop road.

"How do you want it, Willie?" Remo asked. "In the head? Chest? Got a favorite organ?"

"You didn't have to do that to the Eldorado," Willie said. "You know, you're a real sonofabitch."

Suddenly, Willie's head dropped onto the steering wheel of the car. Its wheels bit into a hole and the car's weight pulled it off toward the right side of the road, heading at a marshy field.

With his good right arm, Remo slapped Willie's head away from the steering wheel, then grabbed the wheel and wrestled the car back onto the blacktop. He reached his left leg past Willie's feet and slowly began tapping the brake until the heavy car lurched to a halt.

Remo shifted the car into neutral, then walked around to the driver's side. Willie lay with his head back against the seat. His eyes were open, but Remo realized he was dead.

Remo pulled Willie out of the car and let his body drop heavily onto the road. Then he slid behind the wheel of the car and drove off.

He felt bad about scratching a new Eldorado.